Claimed by the Rebel

Cameron Hart

Published by Cameron Hart, 2024.

CLAIMED BY THE REBEL

First edition. June 5, 2024.

ISBN: 979-8227335135

Written by Cameron Hart.

Want a free book?

Sign up for my newsletter[1] and get your free copy of Chasing Stacy!

One look at the stunning waitress carrying the weight of the world on her shoulders, and I'm a goner. I wasn't looking for a sweet little thing with auburn hair and more baggage than I can fit on the back of my bike, but there's no going back now. She's mine. I'll prove to her I'm more than capable of handling her past and making her feel safe again.

1. https://dl.bookfunnel.com/7wbqvhsx8r

Chapter 1

Razor

"Fuckin' cages," I mutter as I unbuckle my seatbelt and shove it aside. I feel like I can breathe again without that torture contraption wrapped around my chest and torso. Now if only I could punch a hole in the roof for some extra air flow and replace the steering wheel with handlebars, this might not be so bad.

Once I joined Rebel Hearts MC at eighteen, my Harley has been my one and only. My most prized possession. When I'm out on my bike, leaning into a turn, my silhouette slicing through the wind as it whips around me, the world doesn't seem so bad. For those few moments, it's just me, the rumble of my bike, and the vast expanse of the Texas hills.

Being in this steel cage is not only making me claustrophobic but nauseated as well. Unfortunately, I don't have a choice. As the Enforcer for Rebel Hearts, I often scope out leads and analyze the legitimacy and danger of the situation. It's difficult to discreetly collect information on a bike, not only because of the noise but because the bike itself could draw the attention of our potential target and blow our cover.

So... a fuckin' cage it is.

Pulling out my phone, I snap a few pictures of my surroundings, zooming in on the partially rusted road sign across the street and the address of the abandoned-looking farm on the outskirts of town. It's a great location for a clandestine meeting, which is exactly what I'm hoping will happen tonight.

I found the perfect spot to park that keeps the car hidden by the shadow of an overhanging tree limb while still giving me a solid view of the dirt lot, the surrounding shanty farmhouse, and various decrepit structures around the property.

Sighing heavily, I settle in for a stakeout that I hope won't last all night. The lead we got from a new prospect seems legit, but after years in the MC world, I know better than to take a prospect at their word. Some of these shitheads will do or say anything to patch in, including lying and wasting resources by sending the club on an unnecessary mission.

After about ten minutes or so, movement catches the corner of my eye. I turn my attention in that direction, watching as a door to the main farmhouse swings open and bangs against the side of the wall. My eyes narrow as I take in the familiar face of an old rival; Diego Alvarez.

I swallow past the growl stuck in my throat, not wanting to draw attention to myself. Diego is one of a handful of men at the head of this branch of the cartel. If he's here, that means these fuckers are trying once again to get a foothold in this small Texan town. Maplewood is in a unique location that would give the cartel access to huge suppliers and buyers in Dallas. This isn't the first time they've attempted to take over the drug trade and funnel their cocaine through our streets.

My brothers at Rebel Hearts MC won't let that happen. We've faced off with these mother fuckers before, and we'll do it again. There's no vanquishing the cartel, of course. Not yet, anyway. Like a hydra, when you eliminate one branch of the cartel, two more seem to grow back and double down on their previous mission.

Well, not this time.

I continue snapping pictures on my phone, making sure to get clear shots of Diego and his accomplices. Some I recognize, others are fresh faces, ready to take the place of their elders when they are inevitably killed in the line of duty.

Just when I think everyone is outside, the door opens again, revealing something shocking. *Okay, this is a solid lead.*

A member of the Serpents steps outside, followed by another and another. Five in total. Even if I didn't recognize the VP of the Serpents, I would know it's them by the logo on the back of their cuts.

So this is the next step, I think to myself. The cartel has struck up some kind of deal with the Serpents to open the flow of drugs through our town. Not on my fuckin' watch.

I'm too far away to hear anything they are saying, but this is enough evidence right here to convince the club we need to make this our new number-one priority. Checking the clock on the dashboard, I'm pleased to see it's only nine in the evening. Plenty of time to stop by the clubhouse, grab a beer or three, and update the Sergeant in Arms, Drak, about my discovery. Lord knows our President, Aldis, will be at home with his old lady by that point. Tritan and Chance are more than likely already at home with their women.

"Suckers," I scoff to myself. I respect the Pres, Secretary, and Treasurer, of course. They're my brothers and I'll defend them with my life. That doesn't mean I have to approve of every decision they make. It's not the women they chose - Winnie, Bess, and Jessa seem nice enough. It's the whole idea of a *relationship*.

I grimace, unable to even think the word without a visceral reaction. Trust, vulnerability, *sharing feelings*... no, thank you. Then there's the romance part of it. I don't have the slightest clue how to be sweet and romantic, and honestly, I don't care to know.

But, to each their own, I suppose.

I'm about to put my phone away and get the hell out of Dodge when the farmhouse door opens again. I almost don't even bother sticking around, knowing I already have all the evidence I need now, but something pulls my attention back toward the building.

The first thing I notice is a bright streak of long blonde hair, glittering in the moonlight. Every muscle in my body tightens, and I'm frozen in place as if some spell has been cast over me.

When the magical creature turns around and faces my direction, I get a mouthwatering view of her curves silhouetted by the bright light of the moon. I know she can't see me, but I feel... exposed. It's sudden and I don't quite appreciate how this woman has undone me without even trying. Without even knowing I exist. Wasn't I just calling my friends suckers for falling for their women?

My brain and body aren't communicating properly, and I watch myself open up the camera app once again, having no control over my motions. I zoom in on the beauty who is so close, yet impossible and forbidden to touch. I find myself taking picture after picture, trying to capture her essence. Those full, pouty lips, her slightly upturned nose, rounded cheeks, and her long, slender neck that leads down to her chest... which I shouldn't be looking at. What the fuck is wrong with me?

Still, I focus once more on her face, taking in her long lashes and wide eyes. Are they brown? Green? Dark blue? I can't tell from here, and for some reason, that pisses me the hell off. Some insane, unreasonably possessive part of me needs to know. I need to know her story, not just the color of her eyes. I need to know what makes her happy, what scares her, what she wants out of life. *What the hell? What are these thoughts?*

I flip on video mode, hoping to catch the curvy goddess in motion, but then I get an incoming text from one of my MC brothers. I huff out a frustrated breath, hesitating for a moment on whether to read it or not. Eventually, my loyalty to the club wins out and I navigate to my text messages.

Drak, our Sergeant at Arms, wants to know if I have any updates. *Boy, do I ever,* I think to myself. I reply, telling him I'll be at the club soon with a full report.

Before pulling the car away from the curb and making my way to the Rebel Hearts clubhouse, I take one last look at the scene in front of me. What I see has my blood boiling.

The fucking VP of the Serpents, Viper, has his meaty paw wrapped around the blonde woman's arm and he's tugging her inside. He looks like he's reprimanding her, and my cold, dead heart sinks when her shoulders drop and she nods her head in defeat.

Every protective instinct inside me rises up, and I have to clench my hands into fists to keep from ripping the car door off its hinges and lunging at Viper for putting his hands on any woman out of anger, let alone this... this... angel.

Fuck me, I shouldn't be having these thoughts. These desires.

When everyone is back inside, I take my cue to leave. Still, I know I'll be thinking about the blonde beauty all night long.

Chapter 2

Aurora

"Mrghh," someone groans before coughing and then rolling over, resuming their chainsaw-level snoring. A second later, another man leaps up from where he was strewn out on the floor of the clubhouse, barely making it to the bathroom before hurling.

Thus begins another glorious morning here at the Serpents clubhouse.

I survey the damage done to the bar and common areas, sighing to myself when I see it was another wild night. Of course, it was. Every night is a wild night. Especially now that we have a new business partner; The cartel.

A shiver runs down my spine at the thought. I wasn't supposed to know, but I overheard a conversation the other night right outside the farmhouse the Serpents converted into their clubhouse. Curiosity got the best of me, and I walked outside, thinking for some stupid reason I'd find a friend. It gets lonely being the little sister of the Vice President of an outlaw biker gang.

Instead of a new friend or even a passerby who got lost and was in need of some direction, I found my brother with a group of men who looked vicious and ready for a fight. That's saying something, considering I grew up with violent criminals who had brutal tempers and short fuses.

I only heard a snippet of the conversation before my brother grabbed me and dragged me back inside, but it was enough for me to know we were in deep with some bad people. Running drugs is nothing new for the Serpents, but welcoming the cartel into our town? Putting everyone here at risk? It was a shock, even though it really shouldn't have been. My brother wasn't always this way, but it's been so long since I've seen a softer side of him, that I wonder if it exists at all anymore.

Stepping over another MC member passed out on the floor, I head to the bar and grab a bucket and wash rag. I fill up the bucket with soap and water, setting it on the bartop before gathering up a few garbage bags.

I spend the next hour picking up empty bottles and cans, along with food scraps, condom wrappers, and a myriad of other things I really don't want to think about. I learned early on that it's best to wear rubber gloves and a facemask when handling the aftermath of a Serpents party.

Once the garbage is mostly under control, I begin scrubbing tabletops and chairs, scrunching up my nose when I come across certain stains. I don't look too closely because again, I really, truly don't want to know.

This whole lifestyle sickens me. If I had any other choice or thought I'd survive longer than five minutes outside the Serpents compound, I'd have made a run for it years ago. As it is, I'm a prisoner. I cook, clean, and stay out of the way. Anything more, and I'm quickly reminded of my place in the hierarchy - the very bottom. Anything less, and my brother isn't afraid to use a heavy hand to motivate me to get my chores done.

I wipe the sweat from my forehead and let out the breath I was holding. Looking around the bar once more, I'm pleased to see it's mostly back to normal. I'll have to wait to sweep and mop until the men currently passed out on the floor sober up enough to stand, so that means I have a little free time.

After rinsing out the bucket and tossing the dirty rag in the laundry bin for me to wash later, I drag the three large garbage bags through the kitchen and out the back door leading to the dumpster. Hoisting one bag on my shoulder, I roll it up and over the rim of the dumpster, followed by the second bag.

My foot slips right as I'm heaving the third bag onto my shoulder, and I stumble slightly, tipping to the side. I try holding out my arms to help keep my balance, but the heavy garbage bag is too much for me to counteract. Inhaling sharply, I turn my head to the side and put my hands out in front of me as I fall onto the gravel, catching myself with my hands and knees.

"Frick," I curse under my breath. The trash bag that was on my back rolls off, hitting the ground next to me with a thud. Slowly, I lift my hands and readjust so I'm sitting on my butt with my legs out in front of me.

I hiss as I pick out the little pieces of gravel that embedded themselves into my palms and knees. The scrapes on my knees and hands are superficial, but I have a nasty cut on my left elbow from the sharp edge of the dumpster. Of course, I do. What else is new?

I allow myself a few more moments of being outside, even if it's only a trip to the dumpster that ended with me stumbling over my own two feet. That's about as much freedom as I'm afforded these days, aside from the occasional grocery or supply run.

Taking one last deep breath, I push myself up off the ground and hobble inside, heading straight to the first aid kit. I'm all too familiar with its location. If I'm not being "punished" for not doing a good enough job, I'm bumping into things, breaking glass, slicing my fingers, and as I just demonstrated, tripping over nothing. In short, I'm a clumsy trainwreck who needs constant access to bandages and peroxide.

I open the white box, digging through the materials until I come across a large gauze pad and medical tape. Cleaning out and fixing up a wound one-handed might sound challenging to some, but I have it down to a science. I dab some peroxide, gritting my teeth against the sting before placing the gauze pad. I secure one end of the medical tape to the counter to keep it taut, then cut the appropriate length and secure the tape to the top of the gauze pad. This helps keep the wound covered while cutting the rest of the tape.

I'm almost through my routine when Daniella walks into the kitchen, wearing nothing but the oversized Led Zeppelin 80s tour t-shirt of the club member she slept with last night. She's one of a handful of women - club bunnies, they're called - who always hang around in hopes of becoming someone's old lady. Last week it was Tank, the week before it was Remi, and this week appears to be Zep. He got his nickname because he only ever listens to Led Zeppelin, and only at the highest volume.

"What did you do this time, honey?" Daniella asks in her fake sugary-sweet voice. I'm not one to judge women on their sex lives just because I don't have any experience whatsoever. One thing I can't stand though is when Daniella puts on her persona of a ditzy blonde girl with a baby voice.

"Nothing I can't handle," I tell her in my cheeriest voice as I concentrate on securing the last strip of tape onto my bandage.

Daniella shakes her head at me, the familiar look of *not again* written all over her face.

"See? All better," I say, pushing past her so I can put the first aid kit away.

"What are we going to do with you?" she says, her tone partially joking and partially annoyed. I know it's a rhetorical question, but I want to answer, *let me leave. If I'm such an inconvenience, and such a clutz, just let me leave.*

Even as I think the words, I know they'll never be true. I can't leave. I know too much.

I shrug and walk out of the kitchen, not wanting to continue this conversation. When I run smack into Viper, however, I second-guess my decision to leave.

"What the fuck happened to you?" my brother growls, his gaze focused on my elbow.

"Nothing," I say, repeating the same answer I gave Daniella.

"It better be nothing," Viper spits out as he steps around me. "Big news tonight. I'll be calling church later, and I need you to handle food, drinks, and cleanup."

"Like every other night," I mutter to myself.

"You got something to say?" Viper snaps, his eyes latching onto mine. Dark, soulless orbs stare back at me, making my skin crawl. I'm not sure if his dead stare is from a mix of drugs he's coming off of or if he's completely gone, but this isn't my brother. Not anymore.

When did he become so cruel? So uncaring? The boy I knew growing up, my big brother, Chad, protected me from the worst of our parents' criminal activities. He held my hand and distracted me by playing card games and telling me stories. And then one day... he joined them. It was no longer me and my brother against the world. It was the world and my family against me. Chad became Viper and he never looked back.

"I'm talkin' to you, bitch," Viper growls, stepping into my personal space.

"No," I automatically answer. "Nothing. I'll be there tonight, Chad."

"What the fuck did you just call me?!" he growls, bending down so he's nearly eye-level with me.

"V-Viper," I correct myself, scrunching my shoulders up as I take a step back. "Sorry. I meant Viper."

A low snarl rises up from his throat, then he nods and straightens up. "That's right. I'm Viper. The fucking Vice President of the fucking Serpents. Don't you forget it."

I nod and watch my brother walk down the hall and out into the bar area. Only when I'm convinced he's gone do I let out the breath I was holding. It takes a few more moments before I stop trembling, but as soon as I do, I beeline to the bathroom and splash some cold water on my face.

Looking at my red-rimmed, wide hazel eyes, I have to swallow back tears. How did I get here? And more importantly, how do I get out?

Chapter 3

Razor

I slug back the rest of my energy drink before grabbing the binoculars sitting in the passenger's seat. Lifting them to my face, I peer out and survey the decrepit farmhouse and even shittier barns located around the property. Last time, I thought this was simply a meeting place. Now I know it's the Serpents' compound.

It's only two in the afternoon, so I'm not sure that I'm going to see much action. Still, I have to check on things. To make sure there aren't any other secrets we don't know. It has nothing to do with wanting another look at the mysterious blonde woman.

My mind wanders to the photos I took of her that first night. I'd be lying if I said I haven't looked at them a few times. Just three or four times. Maybe five. Nothing obsessive or anything. It's just that she might be involved and I need to know what she looks like. For club reasons.

I may have made a pit stop here yesterday, just to see how things were progressing with the cartel. Did I happen to see the curvy, breathtaking woman with silky blonde hair? Yeah, sure. No big deal.

And so what, I watched her for a bit, mostly to see what, if anything, she knows. I'm not quite sure what role she plays in the MC, but as far as I can tell, she's not anyone's old lady. She's sure as shit not a club bunny. In fact, when I've seen her interact with other club members, she's always stiff and stilted, keeping a solid three feet of distance between herself and whomever she's speaking to.

A surge of jealousy pushes its way into my system, ramping up my heartbeat and sending adrenaline pulsing through my veins. It's as shocking as it is all-consuming. The thought of her with another man... *Fuck*. I don't even know this woman's name. I shouldn't be jealous of a hypothetical man, or jealous of anything about her at all. This mission must be taking its toll on me. That's it. I'm not stalking Blondie, I'm simply doing a thorough job investigating–

The back door of the large farmhouse swings open and I watch with rapt attention as the object of my not-obsession walks out into the sunlight. All other thoughts vanish from my mind as I focus on the lovely, mysterious creature leaning against the side of the old house. She sighs heavily and tilts her head back until it's resting against the siding as well. Her shoulders drop and she closes her eyes, taking another deep breath.

She looks weary. Bone-tired. But there's something else there. Something I can relate to on a fucking visceral level. My girl feels trapped.

Shit. Not *my* girl. Just a girl. A woman. But not mine in any way, shape, or form.

Still, the longer I look at her, the heavier my non-existent heart grows. She looks so fragile in this moment, unbearably vulnerable with her defenses down. The gorgeous woman usually keeps a smile on her face, despite her environment and the assholes she has to deal with every day. Her bright, bubbly demeanor is visible even from fifty feet away. But today? She's broken. Defeated. She's letting it all show, though there's no one to see. No one except for me.

A moment later, she pushes off the side of the house and walks across the gravel lot, heading to a corner on the far southern end of the property. I follow her with my eyes, adjusting the settings on the binoculars to focus in on her movements.

The woman stumbles a bit, though I don't see anything for her to trip on. She wobbles, throwing her arms out to try and maintain her balance. It's too late. She falls, her knees hitting the ground first. She catches herself on the palms of her hands, then hops up again, as if nothing happened.

My heart lurches in my chest, everything in me screaming to jump out of the car and see if she's okay. I mean, what the fuck? She just tripped. It's not a big deal. I shouldn't care at all, let alone this much. At least she's okay.

I continue spying on her through the binoculars, observing as she wipes her hands on her shorts and then brushes the gravel from her knees. The woman starts walking forward again, still picking pieces of loose gravel off of her shirt when she stubs her toe on the corner of a raised garden bed I've been curious about since I first scoped out the compound.

My heart is racing. She hurt herself for the second time in less than a minute. I need to get to her, to help her... but I can't. It would blow my cover, for one, and also, I might terrify the poor woman if I came sprinting out of nowhere to ask if she's okay.

Still... as I watch her bend over and rub her sore toe, a rogue thought crosses my mind. For the first time since joining the MC, I'm actually considering putting my loyalty and everything I've worked for at risk. For what? A woman I've never officially met or talked to?

As I look over at her, the sun weaving through her hair and making it sparkle, I know she's already changed something deep inside me. She's opened up a longing I didn't think I'd ever have and ignited a fire that I know won't be quenched until I taste her lips.

Fuck me, what the hell is going on?

I can't look away, especially when she's giving me a spectacular view of her ass. I shouldn't be looking, and I sure as shit shouldn't be imagining all the filthy things I'd like to do to her. Jesus, I can't remember the last time my cock twitched, let alone became hard. But right now? The blood is rushing to my dick so fast I'm a little lightheaded.

The woman straightens up, her delicate hand reaching out toward the assortment of flowers I don't know the names of. It's a little oasis of color and greenery that attracts butterflies and ladybugs. It's so out of place, surrounded by the dirt and gravel lot. Such rare beauty found in an otherwise desolate place. Much like the mysterious woman herself.

I can't take any more of this. The temptation, the longing, the confusing feelings the curvy goddess brings out in me, plus the fact that she has me questioning my priorities in life... it's all too much. I'm in too deep.

Taking one last look at the ethereal, confounding woman, I finally put the binoculars away and pull out of my spot. This is getting ridiculous and I need to get my head back in the game. No distractions.

I make it all of three blocks before the image of my blonde beauty bending over fills my mind. I'm so fucked.

Chapter 4

Aurora

"Wait, what?!" I exclaim over the phone to my good friend, Beatrix. "Like, a *mansion* mansion? With multiple bathrooms and fifty bedrooms and a library like in *Beauty and the Beast*?"

My friend laughs over the phone, though her tone is surprisingly sarcastic. "No, it's definitely not a fairytale. The place has been abandoned for years, though apparently my great-great-aunt who lived across the country or something had been paying property taxes on it, so... it's just been sitting here, untouched, for over a decade."

"A great-great-aunt?" I ask. Bea and I went to school together from kindergarten through high school, and during that time, she was in and out of foster care homes. Some better than others.

I narrowly miss hitting a lamp post with my elbow and breathe a sigh of relief when I'm able to steady myself and the three bags of groceries I'm juggling in my hands. My purse strap slides down my shoulder and I try doing a circular motion with my arm to try and get it back into place. No such luck.

"I know. Crazy, right? I had no idea she existed until her attorney tracked me down and told me I inherited a piece of property."

"You could have been living with her the whole time instead of..." I trail off, not wanting to bring up unpleasant memories. Plus, it's not helping to rub it in.

"I try not to think about what might have been, you know? Who knows if my life would have been better or worse if I lived with her? Besides, I probably wouldn't have met you, and that would've been a tragedy, don't you think?"

I smile even though I know she can't see. Beatrix has been through a lot in her life, but she still finds a way to focus on the positive.

"Definitely," I reply, adjusting the strap of my purse once again as I stop at a crosswalk.

I finally give in to the fact that I need to juggle some things around and switch arms for my purse. Securing my phone between my ear and my shoulder, I tilt my head at an angle to make sure I don't drop it. I shrug off my purse, then swap hands between the grocery bags and my purse. I'm about to swing the strap of my purse over my other shoulder when my phone slips.

"Oh crap!" I squeak out. The only thought in my mind is that my phone is the single connection I have to the outside world. If I lose or break this one, I have no idea when my brother might get me another one, if ever.

I lunge forward, dropping the bags and my purse on the ground. My phone tumbles off the curb and into the street, while my heart lodges itself in my throat, making it hard to breathe. *If it falls into a sewage drain or gets run over by a car...*

"Gotcha!" I whisper to myself in victory. My fingers wrap around the little device that holds the key to my freedom and I'm able to take a full breath again.

As soon as I grab my phone from its precarious place on the street, someone grabs me from behind, securing an arm around my waist and pulling me back onto the sidewalk a second before a car speeds past, horn blaring.

I gasp, realizing what just happened. Or what almost happened. My heart stutters and then pounds against my chest hard enough that it might crack a damn rib. I try to scream or cry or show some kind of emotion, but no sound comes out.

The immediate danger of the moment has passed, and as things settle in my mind, I realize someone pulled me out of the way. I turn around, though the arm still wrapped around my waist makes it a bit difficult.

I'm met with espresso-brown eyes, staring at me with so much intensity I have no choice but to fall right into his gaze. It's *him*. I mean, I don't know him at all, but somehow... I do. I recognize him, though not his looks. I'd certainly remember someone as striking and rugged as him.

With deep brown eyes framed in even darker lashes, black hair, tan skin, and a strong jawline dotted with stubble, I'm positive I've never seen this man before. Yet I already feel a pull, some sort of connection I've never had before. The longer I stare into those all-consuming eyes, the more I see a pain, a longing, a loneliness that resonates deep within my soul.

He blinks, breaking the trance I was in.

"Ohmygod," I say in a rush once I find my voice. "I... You... And then... zoom! And you... you saved me." I'm still a little out of sorts, which is understandable considering the circumstances. "Thank you. I..."

The man hasn't said a single word, though he still has a tight hold on me. I don't mind. The chiseled muscles of his chest and abs press against the soft curves of my body, sending an unexpected shiver down my spine. For the first time in my life, the presence of a tall, powerful man doesn't terrify me or make me want to run away and hide.

Those brown eyes peer down into mine, though I can't quite place the look swimming in their depths. Right here, in this stranger's arms, I feel safer than I ever have. People scurry around us while cars zip by, but the noise fades to a blur in the background. It's just me and my mysterious rescuer.

The next second, he drops his arm from around my waist and takes several steps back. The man shoves his hands in his pockets and looks down at the ground, muttering something to himself.

"Um, thank you," I say again, putting on my brightest smile. "I tend to be a little clumsy, and then with my purse and groceries and phone... oh! Speaking of..."

I look around for my discarded items, only to have my savior move closer to me and pull me away from the curb with his large hands on my hips. I try not to notice the shock of lightning shooting down my spine or the dull, pulsing ache settling between my thighs, but I have a feeling I'll be obsessing over this interaction for weeks to come. I didn't realize how starved for human contact I was until this moment.

"I'll get it," he grunts. "You stay put."

I frown slightly at his gruff tone, but how can I be anything but grateful at this moment? I send a quick text to Bea letting her know I'm okay and we'll have to finish our conversation later, then I watch the giant beast of a man pick up my purse and hand it to me. He's laser-focused on me as I slip it on over my shoulder. He gathers up the groceries that had spilled onto the sidewalk, and I'm thankful to see everything is still there and in order. Nothing broke, so I won't have to go back to the store.

I hold out my hand for the grocery bags, but the man keeps them secure in his grip.

"Um, so, thank you. Seriously. I've always been accident-prone, but not death-prone," I ramble nervously. He's giving me nothing to work with, so I'm just trying to fill the silence. "I guess practice makes perfect." I wince at my stupid comment while the man crinkles his brow slightly. "Not that I want to die or anything like that. I mean we all have our dark days. But c'mon, death by car has to be a pretty painful way to go. Plus, it can't be a hundred percent success rate, so the results would be hit or miss. *HA*!" I snort out a laugh. "Get it? *Hit* or miss?"

The man is studying me like I'm a foreign species, which is fair. I haven't held a conversation with a non-Serpent member in years, and it shows.

"What were we talking about again? Oh, right. You saving my life. Thank you, again. That doesn't seem adequate enough. Hmm..." I trail off, trying to think of some way to repay him. I've got nothing. "My favorite coffee shop is right up the block. Let me get you a latte and a scone."

As soon as I make the offer, I feel like a complete idiot. Knowing nothing about this man, I can confidently say he doesn't sip lattes or nibble on scones. He looks like he drinks coffee strong enough to chew and has a dozen raw eggs for breakfast.

"Latte?" he asks, the word sounding wholly unfamiliar on his lips.

"Yeah. Or coffee. Or a raspberry mocha with extra whip and chocolate drizzle. Whatever you want, my treat."

Another blank stare.

"I'll take your silence as an unequivocal yes." This earns me the slightest spark in those dark brown eyes, and I won't lie; I love it.

I loop my arm in his and begin walking down the sidewalk, heading toward my favorite coffee shop. I hardly ever get to leave the compound except to run errands here and there. Today, we needed groceries, so I was given some cash and a shopping list. I know better than to run away with the cash. My brother would find me in a heartbeat and make me pay back every penny, by any means necessary.

"This will be fun," I tell my hostage. He shuffles his feet behind me, still holding my grocery bags. "I haven't made a new friend in ages."

The mysterious man makes a strange sound in the back of his throat, but I ignore it. I'm just happy to have someone to talk to who isn't a Serpent or associated with any of that world. Maybe today won't be so bad after all.

Chapter 5

Razor

What the hell is happening right now?

I stare down at the little lady currently pulling my six-foot-three, two-hundred-and-eighty-pound self down the sidewalk. One minute I was on my bike, watching the blonde woman I'm definitely not stalking, and the next minute she dropped her phone and dove in front of a car to grab it.

I had no choice but to act. My mind went completely blank and my sole focus was to get her out of danger. The moment I wrapped my arm around her waist, I knew I crossed a line. And when she turned around and locked her eyes on me? I was done for.

Even after studying her photos and checking up on her these last few days, I wasn't quite sure what colors her eyes were. Sometimes they looked green, while at other times, blue flecks shined through.

But now I know. Her wide, hazel eyes will never leave my memory. Swirls of blue, olive, and brown make up her mesmerizing gaze. I swear there was a hint of recognition swimming in their depths when she first looked up at me. God knows I have nearly every contour of her face memorized, but she's never seen me before now.

Or maybe I'm losing my goddamn mind since a handful of my MC brothers went and settled down with women of their own. *Am I subconsciously looking for a partner?*

That thought has me stopping in my tracks. Literally. The woman whose name I still don't know comes to an abrupt halt with her arm still looped in mine. She teeters on her heels then falls backward. I'm right there to catch her, trying with all of my might to ignore her soft curves and sweet, floral scent.

No, for fuck's sake. Stop this right now, I scold myself. I was only going to look at her from afar. That was the plan. Just follow her around a bit and see if she knows anything or goes anywhere noteworthy. For the club.

At this point, I know I'm just lying to myself. This isn't for the club. It's selfish and dangerous and all for me.

Still, I wasn't going to talk to her, let alone touch her. Now that I have...

"Can you go two minutes without hurting yourself?" I grunt as I help the mysterious woman stand up on her own two feet. The second the words fall from my lips, I wish I could rip them out of the air and swallow them back down.

Her shoulders drop, her entire posture changing so she's folded in on herself. I never want to be the cause of this reaction ever again. She looks ashamed to even take up space, which is so different from the woman I've come to know over the last week of not-spying on her.

I open my mouth to apologize, but my voice won't work. Can't remember the last time I said sorry unless it was sarcastic or insincere. With this precious woman, however, I truly hate myself for making her feel less than.

"I know I'm a bit clumsy," she says, straightening her spine and rolling her shoulders back. "I mean, that's kind of the whole reason we met." Her voice is back to its normal, cheery tone like nothing ever happened.

Her words have my stomach tying itself into knots. She has no idea how we really met and I hope she never finds out. I get the sense she doesn't trust easily. Hell, anyone who has been in an MC on the wrong side of the law doesn't trust easily, if at all.

She peers up at me, a smile plastered on her face despite the way I just snapped at her. I don't want to think about how many times she's been yelled at and harassed at the Serpents' clubhouse and she's had to smile her way through just to survive.

I want all of her smiles, but I want them to be genuine. I want... I want to make her happy. Happy, safe, and fulfilled.

What is wrong with me? Where are these thoughts coming from?

"Anyway," she says, looping her arm around mine once more. "Don't make it weird. I'm just buying you coffee for saving my life. No big deal."

"Seems like a fair trade," I say for some reason.

The curvy little lady looks at me over her shoulder, those hazel eyes sparkling with playfulness. God, what that does to me. I'd play with her. Fuck, I'd love to dive into her sweet body and find all the things that make her tremble and scream out in pleasure.

So goddamn inappropriate.

"Did you just make a joke?" she asks, raising an eyebrow.

I stare blankly at her and shrug. This makes her throw her head back in laughter, the rich sound filling the air as I breathe it in. A smile tugs at the corner of my lips, but I manage to resist it. Barely. When was the last time I felt like smiling?

"It's okay. I won't tell anyone you have a sense of humor," she whispers before giving me a wink.

I let her continue to lead me down the sidewalk until we reach a coffee shop at the end of the block. Once inside, she skips right up to the counter and greets the barista with a friendly smile. How she can be that enthusiastic about anything is beyond me. The energy required to give a shit about anything other than the MC left me years ago. Watching the blonde woman who has captured my attention, however, I think I may just have found a reason to start caring again.

"...And I'm paying for whatever he's getting, too. Whatever he orders, make it a large. Oh, and a cinnamon roll." She looks over her shoulder at me, and I'm caught up once again in her beauty. "You like cinnamon rolls, right?" Before I get a chance to speak, she answers her own question. "Of course, you do. Everyone loves cinnamon rolls."

Truthfully, I've always been neutral on cinnamon rolls and all pastries, for that matter. But now my favorite food is cinnamon rolls.

I order my drink - coffee, black - and stand off to the side to wait for whatever presumably outlandish coffee beverage she ordered.

"So," she says, breaking the silence. "I suppose I should introduce myself. I'm Aurora." She holds out her hand for me to shake and I stare at it, not sure it's a good idea to touch her again.

In the end, I clasp my hand around hers, my large, rough fingers wrapping around her delicate skin. Of course, she has a name like Aurora. Beautiful and ethereal, like the woman herself. I think it's also the name of a Disney princess. A rugged, jaded, old biker like myself has no right to dirty up a princess like Aurora, which only makes her all the more tempting.

"This is the part where you tell me your name," Aurora whispers as if I forgot my line on stage during a play. How is she so adorable? And shit, did I just think the word *adorable*?

"Razor," I choke out. Her eyes widen and she looks down at the counter, then across the seating area in the cafe. I realize she's looking for an actual razor, which is pretty... adorable. "My name is Razor," I clarify.

Aurora's cheeks glow the slightest shade of pink and I get the insane urge to kiss them.

Our drinks are called out, and yup, I was right about Aurora's beverage. It's piled high with whipped cream, caramel drizzle, and mini chocolate chips. Her eyes light up when she sees it, and I vow here and now to get her this drink as often as she wants if it makes her this happy.

Aurora weaves around a few tables until we arrive at a booth tucked away in the corner. I appreciate the privacy. I don't make a habit of coming to coffee shops or really any activity where I have to mingle with the public. For this woman, though, I have a feeling I'll do pretty much anything she asks of me.

She takes a seat and I join her, glad to have my coffee cup in hand so I have something to fidget with. "Is Razor your real name?" Aurora asks, her eyes tinted blue under these lights. Her expression is filled with genuine curiosity and a part of me softens toward her. She truly must not get out much. The entire time I've been observing her, Aurora hasn't left the compound until today.

"Razor has been my name longer than it hasn't," I reply.

Aurora narrows her eyes at me, though there's a grin curling up one corner of her lips. "That's a very mysterious answer, mister," she says in a little sassy voice. "What do you do for a living?"

I hesitate, not wanting to give away all of my secrets. Who knows how she'd react to learning I'm a member of a rival MC. "I'm in the protection and security business," I finally land on. As the Enforcer for Rebel Hearts, that's not technically a lie. It still didn't feel great rolling off my tongue so easily. I don't like lying to Aurora, even if it's a lie of omission.

She nods, then takes a spoon and scoops up her whipped cream topping, licking it from the utensil. My eyes latch onto the movement as I follow her pink little tongue lapping at the cream.

I tear my eyes away from her, willing my dick to calm the fuck down. The woman isn't even trying to drive me insane, but still, I want to taste the cream on her lips and suck her tongue into my mouth until she moans and begs for more.

"Uh, what do you do?" I ask, curious as to how she'll answer.

Aurora pauses for a moment, considering her next words. "I'm a maid and a cook." she finally lands on. "It's for a... private family."

I nod, impressed with how well she took the question. Like me, she's not technically lying. She's also not telling me the whole truth.

"Do you like your job?"

This causes Aurora to freeze, her drink only halfway up the straw to her lips. She blinks a few times, pulling herself out of whatever spiral she was in.

"It's kind of my only option at this point," she says, her words measured. "I don't know that I've ever had the luxury of *liking* my job. It just... needs to be done."

Now, that may be the most honest thing she's said to me all day. She feels trapped, just like I used to be. I knew I recognized a pain so deep inside of her that she doesn't know if she'll ever be rid of it.

I open my mouth to say... I don't fuckin' know. Something. Anything. But then her phone beeps with an incoming message.

I watch as she curls in on herself, her head dipping down while her shoulders hunch up around her ears. I don't have to guess who the text is from. Someone from the Serpents.

"Wow, I, uh, didn't realize how much time has passed. I really need to get back to the... to my job," she finishes as she shoves her phone into her purse. "Sorry to cut this short. Here, you have the cinnamon roll. It's all for you." Aurora pushes the plate containing a giant cinnamon roll the size of her face closer to me. "I know it doesn't come close to showing you my gratitude, I just..."

Her phone beeps again, making her jump. I hate that for her.

"Go on, I wouldn't want you getting in trouble."

She gives me a grateful smile, then grabs her groceries from the seat next to me and takes off. I wait exactly two minutes before walking out the door and following her back to the Serpents compound. I'm in too deep now. I know her name, I know how she smells and how she feels in my arms. It's a terrible idea to pursue anything, and yet...

I pull up to the old farmhouse, putting my bike in neutral and walking it the last block to my well-hidden stakeout spot. As I get settled in for another night of watching over Aurora, I'm already thinking of ways to make her mine.

Chapter 6

Aurora

"Yo, bar wench," someone shouts over the music and chaotic noise inside the clubhouse. "Need 'nother rrrround for the boyssss," he slurs as he lifts an empty beer bottle above his head. Predictably, he proceeds to drop the bottle, letting out a whoop of drunken excitement when it shatters on the ground.

I roll my eyes, hating the nickname. That's what most of the members call me, especially when they're this far into a party. I sigh and pop the tops off of six beer bottles, setting them on a tray and heading toward the table.

"Watch this," one of the guys says.

I barely register his words when he sticks his foot out right in front of where I'm walking. I don't have time to react before my shins hit his boot. I lurch forward, the tray of beer in my hand tilting to the left and then to the right as I try to regain my balance. My foot slips and I tumble over the outstretched leg, finally letting go of the drink tray so I can catch myself on my hands instead of face-planting into the concrete floor stained with god knows what.

The bottles crash around me as the tray hits me in the head and then clatters to the floor. The table of men roars with laughter, a few other members close by joining in.

I'm on my hands and knees, covered in beer and surrounded by broken glass while disgusting, inebriated men jeer at me. How did my life come to this? The worst part is, this isn't the first time I've been made to look like a fool simply for entertainment.

Hot tears sting the back of my eyes but I refuse to let them fall. I won't give them the satisfaction.

I take a moment to gather my wits about me, and then I stand, collecting the fallen tray before walking to the back and grabbing a broom. The sound of broken glass being crunched under heavy boots has me wincing. It's going to be nearly impossible to sweep and mop that area until more people clear out.

Sighing in defeat, I take a second to lean against the back wall and give myself a pep-talk. *You can do this. You don't have another choice. What would life be like outside the compound? You have nothing. No skills. No money. Nowhere to go.*

Okay, so that wasn't so much of a pep-talk as it was a reminder of why I can't afford to leave or yell at those bastards that I'm a person, too. I'm a human being, worthy of respect. At the very least, I don't deserve to be treated that way.

Like so many nights before, I close my eyes and take a deep breath, willing all of the negative emotions down, down, down into the dark shadows of my soul. Only, this time, I can't just forget. Instead, an image of Razor fills my mind, the way he kept his eyes trained on me but not in a way that made me feel gross, like when the guys here look at me. No, when Razor's eyes landed on mine, I felt protected.

Angry, frustrated tears burn my eyes thinking about the injustice of it all. I didn't ask for any of this. I didn't choose this life, I just found myself shoved into an impossible situation and now I'm trapped. Like a rat in a cage living a tortured life until it dies.

A tickling sensation drips down my palm, causing me to look down. A thick, dark red line stretches across my palm, no doubt a cut from one of the many shards of glass scattered around the clubhouse floor. I watch the thin line of blood trickle over my light skin, the contrast mesmerizing.

How many times will I have to endure nights like this? Wounds like this? Humiliation like this?

The back door to the kitchen swings open as Brandi, another club bunny, waltzes in wearing a strapless dress that barely covers her butt. She doesn't even see me as she clomps her way to the bar in her six-inch heels, on the hunt for a biker to make her his, if only for a night.

As the rickety screen door slaps against the frame a few times, an impulsive, reckless thought races through my mind. *Run. Run. Run far, far away from here. From this life. Run until it hurts. Run until you can't breathe. Then, maybe you'll finally be free.*

My feet carry me across the kitchen so quickly and effortlessly I might as well be floating. My mind is still reeling from what's happening, but my body knows exactly what to do. One foot in front of the other, faster, faster, the tread on my old sneakers tearing as I race across the gravel lot, through the uncut grass, then further still, leaping over a pile of logs.

When I land, my right ankle wobbles slightly, but I ignore it and keep going. I scramble up the embankment leading to the ill-kept, rarely-traveled highway on the other side of the compound, my muscles cramping as I gasp for air. The overgrown weeds scratch my legs and arms, but I don't stop. I can't stop now.

A surge of adrenaline and fear washes over my body, pushing me to clear the final row of bushes at the top of the embankment. As I burst through the scraggly branches, my foot catches on a root that's sticking up out of the ground. I throw my arms out in front of me, seeing a flash of concrete and gravel before slamming my eyes shut and preparing for impact.

Only... it never comes.

A hand wraps around my arm and pulls me backward until my back is pressed up against their chest.

"No!" I shout, assuming it's one of the Serpents coming to collect me. "Let me go!" I try throwing my elbow back in hopes of clipping their face or maybe breaking their nose, but the man just holds me still.

"It's me, princess," a familiar voice says calmly.

I stop fighting immediately and go limp in his arms. I don't know why he's here or how he happened to get to me so fast, but right now, I don't care. All that matters is that I have someone here, someone who is on my side. It's been so damn long since I've been able to say that.

Razor gently turns me in his arms so we're face to face. "Aurora," he murmurs, lifting a hand to smooth back my wild hair. "What happened?" His fingers trail down my cheek and across my jaw, those dark brown eyes taking in every inch of my face.

I'm sure I look like a total wreck. Not only do I have leaves and twigs stuck in my hair, but I'm all scratched up and still covered in beer. In short, I feel disgusting, I look even worse, and I have no idea where to go from here.

"I... I... serving beer and then he tripped me... everyone laughed and I... the backdoor was open..." I know I'm not making any sense, but I'm nearly hyperventilating and I'm trying so damn hard to swallow back my tears.

Razor draws me close, not caring about how I smell, the sticky beer, or the scrapes on my face. He folds me into his arms, tucking my head into his chest. For some reason, that caring gesture taps into a deep part of my soul, unlocking the tears I've tried so hard to keep hidden.

"I've got you," Razor murmurs. "I'm right here." One tear falls, then another, until I'm soaking his shirt with every emotion I haven't been allowed to show. "Let it all out," he says softly.

"I can't," I protest weakly. I fist his shirt, not sure if I want to push him away for seeing me like this or pull him closer so I can dissolve into him and have Razor protect me all the time.

His hand covers mine and he gently grazes his thumb over my knuckles until I loosen my grip. "That's it, Aurora," he whispers into the shell of my ear. "Let me hold you. Let me take care of you."

It takes a moment for his words to sink in. "Take care... of me?" I ask with a sniffle. I look up for the first time since my embarrassing outburst of tears, and I'm greeted with a softer look than I'm used to from the stoic man I met a few days ago. His brown eyes peer down into mine and I swear he's mending my broken heart with each beat of his own.

"Yes," he answers with a nod. "Come stay with me." I balk at his suggestion, but Razor continues. "You can regroup and figure out what you want out of life."

He seems to have a deep understanding of what I'm going through and the impact of the decision I just made, though I'm not sure how. "But I can't..." I'm not sure what I'm going to say, I just know the offer is too good to be true. How can this ruggedly handsome, secretly hilarious, surprisingly sweet, Greek god of a man want more of me in his life? I'd just be taking up his space and breaking his stuff with my clumsiness.

"You can," he insists. "All you have to do is trust me. Do you trust me, Aurora?"

Espresso-colored eyes stare down at me, searching my soul for the truth. *Do I trust him?* I've barely spent any time with the man, and yet I can't deny how safe I've always felt in his presence. He's nothing like the men I grew up around, which has to count for something, right?

"I..." Pausing, I look up into Razor's deep brown eyes one last time, knowing this is the moment I give him my heart. "I trust you," I whisper.

"Good," he says right before wrapping me up in his arms again. "That's good, princess. I won't let you down."

It's the second time he's called me princess, and while I'd usually assume it was a sarcastic remark, I like it coming from Razor. He's not malicious or cruel. He saved my life once, and he's about to do it again.

Eventually, we untangle from each other and I wipe the remaining tears from my cheeks.

"Are you okay?!" Razor exclaims, looping his fingers around my right wrist and pulling down so he can look at my hand. I forgot about the initial cut there and must have wiped blood on my face while cleaning away my tears.

"Oh, this is nothing," I tell him as an automatic response.

"You're bleeding," he says flatly. "That's not nothing."

I'm about to tell him I've had worse cuts, but Razor turns on his heel and leads me by the arm toward a car I didn't notice parked across the street from the compound. "Let's get you bandaged up and then we can discuss the next steps. Can't concentrate when you're hurt," he adds as he opens the door for me and clicks my seatbelt in place.

His tone is gruff but his words are impossibly sweet. He wants to take care of me. He's so invested in my health and comfort, that he can't even have a discussion knowing I'm in pain.

As Razor leans back and is about to stand and walk around to the other side of the car, I surprise him and myself by kissing his cheek. Razor freezes, then the tips of his ears turn bright red. Is he blushing? Oh, lordy, I'm in trouble. How is this man adorable on top of his crazy sex appeal and perma-scowl?

I'm not sure how he's going to react, but the next second, Razor presses his lips to my forehead. I'm sweaty and gross and smell like stale beer, but he doesn't care.

We stay like that for a few moments, and then Razor closes my door and runs around to the driver's side before hopping in. I watch the broken-down buildings and faded red farmhouse grow smaller and smaller in the side mirror until the entire compound disappears completely.

I don't know what this next chapter in life will bring, but I hope and pray I'll never be back to the Serpents' clubhouse.

Chapter 7

Razor

I grip the steering wheel with sweaty palms, looking over at the precious woman sitting next to me. Aurora has been silent the entire ride to my place, her forehead pressed against the cool window, and I don't blame her. She just changed the course of her life. She broke free. And I'm so damn proud of her.

I knew something was wrong when I saw my girl burst through the backdoor of the farmhouse, her blonde hair whipping around her face as she ran. I was out on a stakeout, though I've finally admitted to myself that it wasn't for the club. It was for Aurora. I'll never apologize for being there when she needed me most.

Aurora had a frantic, almost manic energy about her, and I hopped out of my car as fast as I could to get to her. My heart wedged itself in my throat when I saw her almost roll her ankle after jumping over a scrap pile of logs. Thank all the gods in the universe that I got to her before she fell onto the unforgiving gravel and concrete.

"Razor?" my girl asks, her voice shaky and tentative.

"I'm right here," I reassure her.

She nods then readjusts so she's leaning over the center console, resting her cheek against my bicep. My heart kicks into high gear at her touch, and I curse this stupid car for not being a motorcycle. If I had my bike, Aurora would be wrapped around me, holding me tight while I weave through the streets and bring us safely home.

We pull into my driveway, but instead of opening the garage door, I leave the car parked outside. I don't know how Aurora would react to seeing a motorcycle in my garage. She's already dealt with so much tonight. It will have to be a conversation for another time.

At least, that's what I'm telling myself to justify not talking about it yet. If Aurora doesn't want to be involved with someone in an MC, that would break my goddamn heart that I just started using for the first time in decades. I'm not lying to her, I'm just... protecting her from upsetting information.

Sounds an awful lot like lying, my unhelpful inner monologue adds.

After helping Aurora out of the car, I wrap an arm around her waist and lead her into my home. She's leaning against me, giving me most of her weight while I direct her down the hall and to the left, where my bathroom is.

We stop in front of the mirror, Aurora's hazel eyes widening when she sees her appearance. With tangled hair, scrapes on her cheeks and chin, and the wild, terrified look on her face, I'm sure she's a little taken aback.

"You're always beautiful to me," I tell her, kissing the top of her head despite the twigs stuck there and the smell of beer.

Aurora shakes her head no, then buries her face in her hands as if she can't stand the image of herself. Another devastating blow to my already heavy heart. My girl has been through hell and back and I know it will take time to undo all the lies she's been told over the years. I just hope she lets me be the one to build her back up.

"It's true," I whisper, gently turning her around so we're facing each other. I remove her hands from where they're covering her eyes, kissing her knuckles before holding her hands in mine. "I'll remind you every single day." I don't know where these words are coming from, but Aurora seems to relax more and more with each one. "Why don't you rinse off in the shower and then I can bandage you up and see what the damage is?"

Again, my girl nods, as if that's all she's capable of at the moment. I take her left hand in mine, examining the original cut I saw there. It's not as deep as I first thought, but I decide to give it a quick cleaning and wrap it in gauze as a placeholder while Aurora takes a shower.

She stands there, her eyes unfocused as she circles her arms around her stomach as if protecting herself from the world. It kills me to see her this way, but I know a shower will make her feel better. Well, maybe not better, but at least more human.

"You're safe here," I tell my girl softly. She doesn't even acknowledge my voice, her mind a million miles away. I can see it all in those magical, multi-colored eyes. "I'm going to turn the shower on, okay?" This time, she nods her head.

Reaching behind her, I turn the water on hot, testing the temperature before standing in front of Aurora again. She's trembling and I'm almost afraid to touch her.

"The shower is ready, baby," I murmur, grazing my knuckles down her arm in the lightest of touches. She flinches, making me want to punch myself in the face.

"Okay," she whispers on a shaky breath.

"I'll leave some of my clothes right outside the door for you to change into. Come find me in the living room when you're ready."

Finally, *finally*, Aurora turns her attention to me, her eyes red and puffy from crying. All of her walls are down, her gaze completely open and vulnerable. I see the lost little girl she tries so hard to hide inside, the trapped woman who longs for freedom, and the defeated, broken angel who has all but given up hope. She has me now, and I'm going to love all the pieces of her wounded soul.

"I'll find you," she says. "Like you always seem to find me." The words hold so much meaning, but my stomach churns knowing exactly why I always seem to find her. Still, my girl is starting to trust me.

Aurora gives me the smallest of smiles, but it still lights up the room. It's a start.

After folding up a pair of sweatpants and a t-shirt and setting them outside the bathroom, I begin pacing around my living room. She's here now. Under my roof. Under my care. *Now what?*

The shower is still running, so instead of wearing a path in my carpet from pacing, I decide to call an old friend. He has more connections than almost anyone I know and more importantly, he's from a different MC. My chest grows tight at the thought of reaching out to someone else to get information on Aurora. Not only would she consider that a breach of the trust I'm trying desperately to earn, but my Rebel Hearts brothers might see it as a betrayal as well.

Still, this is bigger than me. It's bigger than arbitrary club lines, especially when I've been friends with Domino since we were little hood rats who skipped school together. I trust him to keep this confidential.

"Razor? That really you?"

"Yeah, hey Domino. It's been a bit, huh?"

"Ah, what's a few years between friends? Besides, I haven't reached out to you, either. I've been up to my fuckin' eyeballs with all the shit I'm trying to do with turning the club around."

"How's that going?" I ask though I'm kind of in a rush to get to the point of this call. I don't know how much time I'll have until Aurora gets out of the shower.

"The Deviant Souls had some monsters that needed to be eliminated from the club, the president being one of them. Never thought I'd be elected to take over and steer the club in a new direction, but here I fuckin' am."

"You're the best man for the job," I say, though it sounds like a fake platitude even to my own ears.

"So, what's up with you? I take it you didn't call just to shoot the shit."

I wince, though Domino doesn't seem upset. My friend understands sometimes club business takes precedence. "Sorry to cut to the chase, but I don't have much time. I... well... okay, so there's this girl," I start, sounding awkward as hell.

"Oh, wow, okay, this conversation is going in a different direction than I thought. You know that I repel most women with my *charm* and *eloquence*, so I don't know if I'll have any good relationship advice for you."

"I have about a hundred and seventy-three people I'd call for relationship advice before dialing your number," I deadpan.

"I'm just honored I made the list," he replies cheekily. "So, what's this about then?"

I take a deep breath and exhale before thinking of the best way to explain the situation I'm in. "I need information on a... sensitive target." Domino hums in acknowledgment, knowing that *sensitive* means it's a personal favor outside of my MC. One that I don't want to get back to them. "She found herself tangled up with the Serpents."

"Mother fuckers," he growls. We're in agreement there. The Serpents have chapters all across Texas, none of them up to any good.

"She's not a Serpent. From what I can tell, she's some kind of maid-slash-waitress-slash-cook. There's something more though. Can you find out more information? If I dig any deeper, my club will know, and they might not trust Aurora. She's already had such terrible experiences in the MC world. I want her to know not every club is like the Serpents."

"You know I've got your back, but I just want to make sure you know what you're doing. The risk you're taking."

"She's worth it." I give him all the details I know about Aurora and clue him in on the cartel's involvement.

I'm met with silence for a few moments, then Domino says, "Consider it done," and hangs up. I know the search has already started.

I set my phone down on the coffee table and run a hand through my short hair. I have all this... this... energy pent up inside. I'm jittery and nervous but also pumped up and ready to fight off anyone who comes near Aurora. Shaking out my hands and arms, I take a few deep breaths in an attempt to calm the fuck down.

The sound of Aurora padding down the hallway has every muscle in my body tightening, and when she steps into the living room, everything snaps into place. I'm able to take a full breath again now that she's here, my heart finding a steady rhythm as I take in every inch of this precious woman.

Her damp hair is combed out and twisted into a simple braid that hangs over one shoulder. My shirt is huge on her, which makes her all the more adorable. How can I want to cuddle Aurora and kiss the tip of her nose while also wanting to see her bent over the couch, taking all of me as I sink into her from behind?

My eyes roam down her ample chest, rounded stomach, thick thighs... that are bare. She's only wearing the shirt, which is giving me all kinds of inappropriate ideas.

"Come in, princess," I say soothingly, sitting on the couch and patting the spot next to me. Never thought I'd be one to use pet names, but princess is just too perfect. My beautiful, ethereal princess who has been locked away from the world.

She takes a tentative step forward, then another, before she's standing in front of me. "Thanks for the clothes. The pants were too big."

"It's okay, baby. Come sit down and let me look at that cut." Aurora does as I say, though her movements are unsteady and jerky. "Hey," I whisper, reaching out to tuck a few strands of loose hair behind her ear. Aurora hits me with those hazel eyes, a little more green than blue at the moment. She's fidgeting and anxious, two things I don't want her to be when she's with me. "You're safe here," I remind her, not for the first time.

"I, well, I... I don't think you know what you just got yourself into," she says, her voice barely above a whisper.

"So, tell me." I try giving her my best smile, but it's pretty damn rusty. I probably look more deranged than anything else. I grab the first aid kit that I retrieved from the kitchen earlier, open it up, and pull out the appropriate supplies. I don't push her to talk, knowing she'll give me another part of her story when she's ready.

Kneeling in front of Aurora, I gently lift her left hand and remove the gauze I had wrapped around it earlier. I clean the wound out again and this time secure it with a proper bandage before assessing the other scratches. I notice an old, less-than-sanitary bandage pressed over her elbow, and I look up at Aurora with an eyebrow raised in question.

She darts her eyes away from me, a red blush creeping into her cheeks. "Yeah, I guess you should know I'm pretty clumsy. And accident-prone. I'm not..." Aurora sighs heavily, her shoulders dropping in defeat. I hate seeing her this way. "I'm not fun to be around. I'll just break your stuff, trip on something, or more likely, knock everything off tables and shelves with my giant hips."

My gaze immediately drops to her hips, and fuck me, I can't wait to wrap my hands around them and hold her steady while I saw in and out of her sweet, tight little pussy. Clearing my throat, I shake my head and dispel my lustful thoughts. For now.

"Aurora, you're not a burden for existing," I tell her as I remove the old bandage on her elbow and sanitize the cut. She shrugs at my statement and I move on to cleaning up a cluster of cuts from the bushes she ran through earlier.

When I'm satisfied that my girl is all cleaned up and put back together, I take a seat next to her on the couch. Aurora looks up at me, her wide, round eyes brimming with tears. I slowly lift my hand to her face, not wanting to startle her. She lets me wipe her tears away with the pad of my thumb, her gaze never leaving mine.

"I'm not just clumsy," she whispers, nibbling on her bottom lip. "I work for a... well, they're not exactly a legit business," she starts, though I know she's choosing her words very carefully.

I don't say anything, I simply lift my arm over the back of the couch, letting Aurora snuggle up against me. I hold her close, pressing a kiss to the top of her head. I love that she smells like me. My girl will tell me everything in time. And if she doesn't, I have someone on the outside working to help me figure things out as well.

"Have you heard of the Serpents?" she asks. "They're a motorcycle club."

I bite the inside of my cheek to keep from telling her that yes, I'm very aware of every Serpent in town. Instead, I nod. "Yeah, that sounds familiar," I reply, trying to play it casual.

"I'm sure whatever you heard was only the tip of the iceberg. The awful things they do, the people they work with, not to mention the disgusting members themselves..." She trails off as if thinking about a particular incident. Possibly the one that happened tonight. "Now that I'm gone, I don't ever want to go back. I don't want anything to do with the MC life. "

My heart sinks at her words. It's understandable, considering she grew up in arguably the worst MC in the state. Still, I want Aurora to see that not every club is like that. We respect our community and are involved in local charity runs. Yeah, we skirt around the law sometimes, but we have a strict code of ethics. One of which is not running drugs. It's a constant battle to keep Maplewood clean, and now with the cartel trying to set up a trade route, the stakes are higher than ever.

"How did you find yourself working for them?" I ask as I stroke my fingers up and down her bare arm.

"My dad was a member back in the day. He and my mom were..." Aurora takes a deep breath and blows it out, making the few strands of hair framing her face fan out around her. "They were meth addicts. They cooked for the club and then kept a little on the side to feed their own habits."

"I'm so sorry," I tell her truthfully. I can relate to strung-out and absent parents.

"It is what it is," she says with another defeated shrug. I get the sense she's had to repeat those words to herself hundreds of times over the years. No more. I vow to give Aurora the freedom she longs for. "Honestly, having my older brother there to protect me saved me from the worst of it. Well, until he joined the family business."

"No," I murmur, nuzzling into the side of her neck. My woman has been alone for so long, a true, rare gem hidden in a world of drugs, danger, and violence.

"My brother, Chad, used to take me out to the park or to the swimming pool when we were kids. I didn't realize until we were older that he was trying to keep me out of the trailer park while my parents were cooking meth." Aurora's lips pull into a surprisingly soft, nostalgic smile. "We would play hide and seek in the surrounding forest whenever Mom and Dad got into a bad fight. Chad really did try to protect me from the worst of it."

"What happened?" I ask softly. Obviously, Chad isn't there anymore to protect her, otherwise she wouldn't be in this position.

"At some point, he was no longer interested in playing with me or protecting me. My parents introduced him to the family business of cooking and running drugs for the Serpents, and that was that. He's never been the same. When our trailer burned down with our parents trapped inside, Chad had full custody of me when he was just eighteen. We went to live with the Serpents, where my brother continued to cook. He tried forcing me to help, but I couldn't. Even when..." Aurora cuts herself off as she tenses up, a shiver running down her spine. I hate that she has so many painful memories. "I just couldn't," she finishes.

"So instead of cooking meth, they had you cook food and be an all-around servant?"

Aurora nods, then melts against me, letting go of every damn thing now that she's poured out her soul to me. I know I need to tell her about me, about the Rebel Hearts, and how we're nothing like the MC she's experienced.

"I have to ask," I say quietly. "Are any of the Serpents out looking for you?"

Aurora shakes her head. "Honestly, it's already after eight, which means everyone is too drunk and/or high to notice much. They probably won't even come to until noon tomorrow. I'm safe. For now."

"Forever," I correct her. She gasps, nibbling on her bottom lip again. It's too tempting, the way she's looking up at me, those wide, vulnerable eyes filled with equal parts hope and doubt. She wants to be loved so desperately, but she doesn't know how. I hardly know either, but I'll figure it out.

I lean forward, lust and longing warring with decency and not wanting to pressure her or take advantage of her situation. Aurora tips her chin up, her long lashes framing those magical hazel eyes.

"Are we going to kiss?" she whispers. Her innocent question is almost my breaking point.

"Would you like that?" I rasp, shaking with the need to consume her, body and soul.

"I..." A blush creeps up her neck and into her cheeks, but she never breaks eye contact with me. "I've never kissed anyone, but I think... I think I'd like to kiss you."

Her words sink down into my soul. She's never kissed anyone? Does that mean I'll be all of her firsts?

I cup the back of her neck with my hand, my fingers weaving into the silky strands of her hair. Brushing my nose against hers, I give Aurora one last chance to pull away. When she hums in contentment, I close the distance between us, our lips meeting for the first time.

She's soft and sweet, her lips pliant as they part for me. I start out slow, savoring everything about this moment as I suck on her top lip, then bottom lip, before sliding my tongue inside her hot little mouth. Aurora lets out a quiet moan, encouraging me to continue. I lick the roof of her mouth and then suck on her tongue, breathing in everything about my girl as we get lost in our pleasure.

When we finally break apart, my girl's lips are swollen, her cheeks are flushed, and her eyes are glazed over as she blinks up at me.

"How was your first kiss, princess?" I ask, rubbing my nose against hers.

She smiles then presses her lips to mine in a kiss that's all too short. "Perfect," she murmurs dreamily. My heart soars knowing I satisfied my woman in this way.

Aurora yawns, making me chuckle. I kiss her forehead and get her settled back down on my chest.

My sweet girl yawns and tucks her head under my chin. I hold her close, silently promising to never let her go. I'll find a way to keep my girl and my club while also taking down the Serpents. No pressure or anything.

Aurora's gentle snores bring a smile to my face. I'll be right here when she wakes up.

Chapter 8

Aurora

Running, running, running...

Heart racing. Lungs burning. Muscles cramping.

Branches reach out, clawing at my skin and trying to ensnare me further into darkness.

He's chasing me. They all are. My feet pound the forest floor, but all I can hear are the growing number of Serpents members behind me. I know I shouldn't look, but I can't help it. Peering over my shoulder, I see a pack of monsters masquerading as men. The momentary distraction causes me to stumble and trip.

As I roll onto my back, I cover my face, though I still see hands reaching out toward me...

"I'm right here, Aurora," someone says. "You're safe here. You're with me."

I jerk awake, every muscle in my body pulsing with tension.

"That's it, baby. You're safe," he says again.

"Razor?" I ask weakly, my mind still pulling itself from the terror of my dream.

"I'm right here," the deep, familiar voice replies. He strokes my back in a calming motion, his touch bringing me back into reality.

I'm at Razor's house, under his protection, for some reason. I still don't know what he sees in me or why he wants to help. I have a bunch of other questions as well, like how he was right there when I needed him most. Not only when I almost got hit by a car, but earlier tonight when I ran from everything I've ever known.

None of that matters right now. All I can think about is the kiss we shared before I apparently fell asleep. I don't even remember closing my eyes, but I was clearly out long enough to get sucked into a nightmare.

"Sorry," I mumble, still groggy from my impromptu nap.

"There's nothing to apologize for, princess," Razor says, his voice calm and in control.

I look down at his chest where I was all curled up, mortified to see a drool mark there. "Sorry," I say again. "I slept on you for hours."

"It was about forty-five minutes," he says, giving me a small wink. Is this the same man I met a few days ago? "And there's nowhere I'd rather be. Holding you is my new favorite activity."

"You can't possibly mean that," I say dismissively, even though I want his words to be true with every beat of my heart.

"I can, and I do," he replies. "You, Aurora, are worthy of taking up space. You don't have to apologize for existing," he murmurs. His words echo in my mind, though I can't quite accept them.

"But... I'm..."

"A warrior," he finishes for me. I furrow my brow, not expecting that. "You're stronger than you know. Beneath that strength, is a fragile heart I want to protect, if you'll let me."

"Why?" I've asked this before, but he hasn't given me an answer I understand yet.

"You are valuable. Precious. Every new piece of your story you give me only draws me closer to you."

"Me?" I whisper, tilting my head up so our noses are almost touching.

"You," he says meaningfully.

"How–"

Razor cuts me off with a kiss. He cups my face and holds me still while he drinks down my protests. We're both gasping for air when we finally break apart.

"You are everything I never knew I needed," he tells me, his breath tickling my lips. Razor's deep brown eyes sparkle with little golden flecks, his face softening as he holds my gaze.

"You... want me?" I squeak out. I realize I sound like a broken record, but I just can't wrap my mind around everything that's happened in just a few short days. I met this man a week ago and now...

Razor chuckles and leans down, his forehead resting on mine. "You don't seem to believe my words, so why don't I show you how much I want you?"

I barely get the chance to agree before his lips are on mine again. The kiss is slower this time, more deliberate and focused. Razor slips his hands under the hem of my shirt and teases me with light, barely-there touches as he sips from my mouth, drawing out a soft moan from somewhere deep inside of me.

He continues trailing his massive hands up my body, inching my shirt up as he goes. Razor brushes his thumbs across the underside of my breasts, causing an unexpected shiver to run through me.

Razor groans into our kiss, the vibrations running through me and settling in my lower belly, creating an intense pressure. His tongue slowly drags across the roof of my mouth, making me whimper as he pulls away. I automatically follow him, wanting more of this slow burn.

He smirks at me, his eyes growing dark and heavy with desire. "Patience, beautiful. I'll give you everything, but I'm going to do it my way." Razor untangles himself from me, standing up and holding out his hand. "Will you give me control, Aurora?"

I look up at him, the fog of lust clearing just enough to consider his question. I've been controlled my whole life. It's only recently I realized how much. Only leaving the compound to run errands, cleaning the clubhouse from top to bottom every day under threat of violence, and being made to feel like my presence is unappreciated at best, and unwanted at worst... I shouldn't be so willing to jump into something with a man asking me to give up control. Still, my first instinct is to fall into Razor's arms and tell him he can do whatever he wants to me.

Sensing the war raging inside, Razor's eyes soften ever so much. "Giving up control is its own kind of freedom if you trust the person you're giving it to. Do you trust me?"

He's asked me that before, and each time my first thought is yes. I trust him with all of me. "I trust you, Razor," I whisper, taking his outstretched hand. He pulls me up so we're face to face, and then Razor breathes me in before placing a sweet kiss on the side of my neck.

He inches my shirt up once again, higher and higher until he finally lifts it over my head. His lips immediately latch onto my breast, sucking at my nipple and rubbing his tongue on the sensitive peak.

"So fucking beautiful, Aurora. So beautiful when you give in to me. So beautiful when you let me love you like this."

Love? Did he say love?

Before I can even process his words, Razor pulls away from me. Did he mean to say that? Is he freaking out? Does he...

My world turns upside down – literally – as Razor tosses me over his shoulder like I weigh nothing. I shriek and then laugh, kicking out my legs. Apparently, he's unfazed by what he just said. I'll have time to worry about it later. Right now, I need his touch more than I need his answers.

Razor tosses me down on the bed, making my extra weight jiggle. I cover up my belly, the familiar rush of self-doubt rushing through my system. How could I possibly measure up to the shredded, sexy, beastly man standing before me?

He growls before he kneels over me with one knee on the bed. Razor grabs my wrists and pins them above my head with one of his massive hands, while the other hand slides down my body, tracing the contours of my chest, my torso, and my rounded belly.

"You're perfect. Thought I made that clear. I guess I'll have to show you that, too, Aurora," he whispers into my lips.

I think he's going to kiss me, but instead, Razor rubs his nose against mine before trailing his lips and nose down my neck, over my collarbone, between my breasts, and lower, lower, lower...

He nips at the soft flesh of my belly, sending a jolt of electricity to my throbbing clit, followed by a warm rush of wetness dripping out of my pussy. Razor takes a deep breath and lets go of my wrists, sliding the rest of the way down my body so he can focus on my pussy.

"I fucking *smell* how much you want me," he growls, spreading my thighs apart and running his nose up and down my slit. I close my eyes, not sure what to do with his attention. Some animalistic sound rumbles out of him. I can feel his need as it vibrates through me, making my nipples and clit ache. I feel my channel clench as more of my arousal leaks out.

Razor growls hungrily as he slides his tongue up and down my pussy, parting my folds. I force my eyes open and look down at his muscular back, rippling and flexing as he devours me. His tongue is everywhere at once – in my entrance, traveling through my folds, swirling around my clit. It's everywhere, and it's consuming me completely. It's all I can focus on. The intense feeling. The wet, smacking sounds. The pressure and heat.

It makes me even hotter knowing he's loving this. The greedy way he's grabbing my ass, the hungry, desperate groans, the eagerness for more. It's all showing me how much pleasure he gets from this. His rough palms slide to the back of my knees and he shoves my legs open wider, pinning them to the bed so he can sit back and stare at me. Razor growls and dives back in, licking me with fury, pushing deeper, harder, faster.

I reach down and tangle my fingers in his hair, pulling and pushing him away in equal measure. I can't decide if it's too much or not enough. Not that Razor gives me a choice in the matter. I gave up control and now I have to trust him to take care of me.

Razor lifts his head briefly, locking his gaze on mine. God, he looks possessed. Feral, even. Did I really do that to him?

"Yeah, beautiful," he grunts. "You did this to me."

My cheeks heat up with embarrassment. I hadn't meant to say that out loud, but Razor seemed to like it. He dips his head back down, this time sinking his teeth into my inner thigh, first one, and then the other, before licking away the sting.

"Oh shit..." I breathe out, spreading my legs wider for him.

"You like that? Like when I mark you? Like knowing you belong to me and no one else?"

I whimper and nod my head, unable to form words at the moment. I want to be his. I want him as my own, my one and only.

Without warning, Razor throws one of my legs over his shoulder, and then the other, before flattening his tongue and licking every part of me. My back bows off the bed as I shove more of my dripping, needy cunt into his face. I can't help it. The way his warm, soft tongue laps at my wetness and then circles my clit has me practically fucking his face.

His hands slide under my ass and grip me there, his fingers digging in deeper with each rough stroke of his tongue. He's helping me find my rhythm as I rub my greedy pussy against his mouth.

"R-Razor, please..." I gasp, clawing at the sheets and snapping my thighs around his head.

He grunts and focuses his attention on my clit, rubbing tight circles around my swollen button with his tongue. I can't stop the breathy moans falling from my lips repeatedly, each one louder than the last as my muscles lock up and my pussy quivers around his tongue.

I teeter on the sharp edge of ecstasy, wanting to savor the aching pressure as it builds. When Razor scrapes his teeth against my clit, pleasure slices through me, unleashing my pent-up need in one vicious explosion.

I cry out and lift up off the mattress, unable to contain the painful bliss rippling through every cell in my body. Wave after wave crashes into me in such rapid succession I don't have time to catch my breath before I'm drawn under once again.

Razor pushes me back down onto the bed with one large hand spread out over my belly, making me take all of what he's offering. My skin burns between my thighs where his stubble is scraping me, but it only serves to heighten the pleasure taking over my body.

Finally, *finally*, I start to come back down. I'm a shaking, sweating, puddle of satisfaction. My legs fall from Razor's shoulders as he stands up and pulls out his dick.

Holy fucking fuck. I mean, just...

"I'm not fucking you today, Aurora. But I need this," he grunts, stroking his massive cock. Jesus, why is that so hot?

I nod my head and spread my legs open for him, seeing his need and wanting to meet it. Razor groans and stares at me, jerking himself off to my naked, exposed body. I watch in awe as his massive shaft grows even longer and then swells up. Razor hisses and throws his head back, pumping his fist furiously.

When he tips his head back down to look at me, his eyes have gone completely black. He bares his teeth and clenches his jaw before stepping closer and pressing the tip of his cock against my clit.

I gasp at how incredible it feels having his hot, hard dick rubbing against me. Razor lets out a roar as he comes on my pussy, releasing his seed in forceful jets against my clit. An unexpected orgasm rips through me. It's short but so damn intense I see black spots in the corners of my vision.

"That's it, that's so fucking it," Razor groans as the last of his pleasure fades.

He falls on top of me, catching himself on his forearms so he doesn't crush me completely. His lips are on mine, giving me a taste of my own release, even as I feel his drip down my pussy. When Razor pulls back, I see his chin glistening with my cum, which makes me lean up and kiss him again. I lick his lips and then plunge my tongue into his mouth, swirling it around his until the adrenaline and lust of my orgasms finally start to dissipate.

"Fuckin' hell, princess," Razor breathes out, his voice raspy from trying to catch his breath. His chest rubs against my sensitive nipples, making me wiggle beneath him. "That was incredible."

"Isn't that supposed to be my line?" I ask with a cheeky grin.

Razor has a comeback on the tip of his tongue, but my stomach lets out an embarrassingly loud grumble. He frowns while I blush.

"I should have fed you," he says more to himself than to me. "I'll do better," he continues. "I can take good care of you, I promise."

This man. How did I find him? Oh, that's right. He found me.

"I think you're doing a pretty good job of satisfying my needs," I say with a wink.

Razor grins and leans in for another kiss, but my stupid stomach rumbles again. "Food first, then we can play later." He presses his lips to mine in a short and sweet kiss, then crawls off the bed and walks his naked ass to the bathroom, presumably to wash up. No complaints here. The view is incredible.

Chapter 9

Razor

Something pulls me from the deepest sleep I've ever had. I groan, not wanting to wake up just yet. Not when I have the sexiest, sweetest, curviest woman in bed next to me.

My phone vibrates from where I left it on the side table last night and I grab it before the noise wakes her up. When Domino's name flashes across the screen, I know I need to answer. Even if it's only six forty-five in the goddamn morning.

"Domino," I answer in a hushed voice as I crawl out of bed and throw on a pair of sweatpants. "You got something for me?"

"You're not going to like it."

I wait until I'm out in the living room to continue the conversation. "Lay it on me," I say, bracing for bad news.

"Your girl isn't just connected to the Serpents. She's the VP's sister."

"Fuckin' Viper?" I ask in disbelief.

"Yup," Domino confirms.

I curse under my breath again and run a hand through my hair before rubbing the back of my neck. "No wonder she feels like she can't leave," I say more to myself than to my friend.

After a moment of silence, Domino continues. "Not sure how much of this you've already figured out, but Aurora grew up in a trailer park on the outskirts of town, near the Serpents' clubhouse. They cooked meth for the club once they became members, then died in an explosion about a decade later. The news report about the incident claimed a gas leak was the problem, clearly trying to cover up the fact that it was a meth den. Neither the media nor the local government wanted anyone to know about how bad the drug problem had become in Maplewood."

"She told me most of that," I reply. I'm thankful my girl shared her story with me so I don't feel *quite* as bad getting a dossier on her from Domino.

"I know you didn't ask for my help with the cartel, but if they're already in Maplewood, they'll be headed my way next."

I grunt in understanding, though he's right, I didn't ask for his help.

"Anyway," Domino goes on. "They've been burnt before from different outlaw clubs or shady businesspeople, as well as run out of town on more than one occasion."

"Yeah, we're no strangers to standing up to the cartel," I say with a hint of pride in my voice. "The Rebel Hearts are dedicated to keeping our town clean of all that shit, whether it's meth or cocaine."

"All that to say, this partnership is still very tentative." I nod even though he can't see me. I know all of this from my own club, but I appreciate the thoroughness my friend took on gathering his intel. "My sources say the cartel will do a few test runs with whoever they're doing business with. They want to make sure the product doesn't get stolen or tampered with and to see if their partner skims any money off the top. More importantly, the partner doesn't know anything about the tests."

"So intercept the first run and we'll put a wedge between the Serpents and the cartel," I say, finishing his thought for him.

"That's my advice," Domino agrees. "Shit," he curses, his voice sounding a bit faded as if he's pulling his phone away from his ear.

"Everything okay?"

"I got another call comin' in. I'm scouting out locations for a new clubhouse. Fresh start, new place, all that shit." He takes a breath and blows it out in frustration. "This real estate agent is busting my balls over here," he grumbles.

"I find that hard to believe. The Domino I know? He doesn't let anyone walk all over him."

"Apparently the only exception is if they wear sparkly pink four-inch heels," he grunts under his breath.

"What?"

"Nothing. Gotta go, buddy. We'll talk again soon."

As soon as we hang up, I navigate over to the app we use at the club to send secure messages. It scrambles the signal and changes the location and metadata each time we use it so it's nearly impossible to track.

I convey the info I got about the test runs, though I leave out any mention of Aurora and her connection to the Serpents. I convince myself it's for the best, but the feeling in the pit of my stomach tells me I'm going to have to tell the truth to everyone soon. I can't live like this much longer.

After sending the message to Aldis, our president, I set my phone on the counter, making a note to charge it later. It's almost dead, but I have more important things to attend to at the moment.

I quietly open the door to the bedroom, smiling when I see my gorgeous woman still sleeping, the morning sun kissing the curve of her hip where the blanket slipped off. Unable to stay away any longer, I strip down once more and crawl into bed next to my precious girl.

Aurora blinks her beautiful eyes awake as I slide under the covers next to her. She turns to face me, giving me the sweetest, sleepiest smile. Her cute, round cheeks turn pink, and I know right here and now that I want to wake up next to this angel every day.

"Morning," I say, watching her blush turn from pink to red.

"Morning," she whispers, biting that bottom lip of hers.

I grip her chin lightly and pull her lip from between her teeth. When I see the fire in her eyes, I don't hesitate to lean down and suck her lip into my mouth, pulling back slowly, then diving into her sweetness with everything I am. I know I need to back off and take it slow, but the way she grips my shoulders and whimpers into my mouth lets me know she needs this as much as I do.

I can't get enough. I'm a desperate, thirsty man, and Aurora is the only one who can give me what I need. I slide my hand over her waist and the curve of her hip, gripping the soft flesh of her thigh and draping her leg over my hips.

"Razor," she moans, tilting her head back so I can suck on the soft skin of her neck.

"Yeah, beautiful?" I murmur, nipping at her pulse point. I growl when she shivers, and then I bite down a little more forcefully.

"Oh, god!" she almost yells, her pussy rubbing against my thigh where I have it nestled in between her legs. "More," she whispers against my mouth. Her little tongue darts out and runs across my bottom lip, teasing me, challenging me, driving me fucking wild.

I roll over, flipping Aurora on her back as I tower over her. Nuzzling into the side of her neck, I trail kisses down her slender column all the way to her shoulder, loving the way she writhes beneath me.

"Yes," she whimpers, thrusting her beautiful tits towards me. She never got dressed from our... *activities* last night, a fact I've been painfully aware of since curling around her naked body hours ago.

Jesus, her breasts are exquisite. Round, firm, more than a handful. I lick one pebbled nipple and then the other, loving her throaty moans and gasps of pleasure.

I suck on one breast, lightly scraping my teeth over her sensitive skin while squeezing her other breast in my large hand. I switch back and forth, kneading, licking, biting her tits until she's shaking underneath me. I could spend hours doing this, exploring her breasts, seeing if I can make her come from this alone. But I have more important things to do right now. Like getting another taste of my angel.

I look up into her hazel eyes, the shade of dark greenish-brown letting me know she's just as into this as I am. Aurora gives me a wicked smile, taunting me, daring me, making my control snap.

I return her lustful gaze, then lean down and start kissing over her torso, her soft belly, her creamy, thick thighs, and finally, over her dripping wet pussy.

I swear to fucking God her sweet and spicy nectar is a drug. I'm addicted, desperate, shaking in anticipation of my next hit. Aurora bucks her hips, getting a little desperate herself. I chuckle darkly, dragging my tongue up and down her delicious little cunt.

"Razor," she groans, the sound making my cock angry with the need to be inside of her.

I'm about to respond, but then I watch a drop of her cream leak out of her pussy and my mind goes blank. Her pretty pink folds glisten for me, her little clit engorged and begging for my tongue, my teeth, the rough pads of my fingers.

I fall right into her pussy, diving tongue first into her sweet heaven. She cries out and falls back onto the mattress, twisting the bedsheets in her fists. I grunt and slide my hands under her ass, gripping her tightly and lifting her up to my mouth so I can feast on her.

Each stroke of my tongue coaxes out another jagged moan, her hips rocking against my face as I eat her out. An urgent need rises up inside of me, something I've never felt before. It's overwhelming me as I dry fuck the bed, sucking on her clit and listening to her moan.

I need to mark her flesh and make her mine. The thought consumes me as I grip her thighs and pull her legs as far apart as they will go, flicking and sucking her clit until her hands find my head, pulling my hair and grinding herself onto my face.

She twists and arches off of the bed, her body shaking with the need for release. She tenses and trembles as she comes in a violent wave. Aurora drenches my face as I swallow down every drop of her orgasm, my own hips rubbing my cock against the bed, searching for relief.

"More," I growl into her pussy.

Aurora is still spasming and writhing on the bed as I stand up and fist my cock, pumping up and down once, twice, three times as I stare down at the goddess spread before me.

"Yes!" she cries out, opening her legs wider and pushing her tits together like a fucking sex goddess.

I can't come, not yet. Not before we've even begun. Pinching the tip of my angry swollen dick, I hiss as precum leaks into my hand. The need to mark her rises up once more, and I reach out, rubbing my cum into the soft flesh of breasts, that one word echoing in my head. Mine. Mine. *Mine.*

"Razor," she says on a shaky breath. I worry it was too much for her, my caveman behavior and intense need to have my mark on her skin.

I lie down next to my sweet girl, ready to apologize for losing my goddamn mind. But Aurora surprises the fuck out of me when she rolls on top of me and punishes me with her kiss.

I let her have control for now. Her tongue slides against mine as she rubs the slit of her pussy against my abs. Jesus, feeling her wet heat on any part of me has my dick pulsing painfully with the need for release. Aurora pulls back and sits up, still straddling my torso. Her lips are swollen, her hair is a mess, and her skin is covered in a thin sheen of sweat. She's never been more beautiful.

My angel traces her fingers over my tattoos, following the swirls of ink in a feather-light touch that makes my cock throb as I adjust her slightly so my dick is trapped in between our bodies. Her dripping folds part for me as I nestle my aching shaft there. My hands roam up and down her thighs and hips, subtly rocking her against me and keeping us both on edge as she explores what's hers.

When Aurora reaches a nasty scar on the side of my ribs, she gasps softly and then leans down and kisses the raised skin. Over and over she finds old wounds and kisses them. She doesn't ask where they came from, she only offers her soft lips and gentle touch. Fuck, she's everything. Every goddamn thing I didn't know I was missing.

She scrapes her teeth across my nipple, making me hiss out a breath. I love that she can be this sweet little thing one minute and a dirty minx the next. It drives me crazy and I need to claim her juicy cunt once and for all.

I thread my fingers through Aurora's hair and tug on the strands, pulling her up toward me. She smiles at me, her eyes filled with equal parts lust and wonder. I fucking love that I'm going to be her first. She hasn't said it in so many words, but if I was her first kiss...

The thought consumes me and I lean up and bite her big, puffy bottom lip before thrusting my tongue in her mouth and sucking the air right out of her lungs. She gasps as I flip her on her back again and glide my impossibly hard cock through her folds, the head tapping her clit with each gentle thrust.

"Razor," she moans again, her nails digging into my biceps. My name on her lips has me close to the fucking edge already. How can one person be so utterly devastating to my self-control?

"Tell me what you need," I rasp into the shell of her ear. "I'll give you anything. Everything."

Hazel eyes lock onto mine, our souls connecting on a level I never knew existed. "I want you to show me what it means to be yours. Completely," she whispers. "I want it all with you, Razor."

I dip my forehead down to touch hers, pausing to take in this moment right here. The moment before the beginning of everything. "I'll take good care of you. You'll never want anyone else," I murmur, rubbing my nose against hers.

"Never," she agrees, her breaths growing shallow.

A wave of pleasure ripples through my body and my balls draw up tight. Fuck, I'm not going to last very long once I'm inside her. She shudders and closes her eyes, her pussy lips fluttering against the sensitive head of my cock.

"Look at me," I command. Her eyes snap open, their hazel irises a stormy gray, clouded over with lust.

Slowly, I press myself into her tight little opening, trailing my right hand up and down her curves, tweaking her nipples and kneading the soft flesh of her hip, encouraging her to move with me. I slide my hand to her center, circling her clit with my thumb.

Aurora gasps and opens up a little more for me, her juices helping me slide deeper inside her.

"That's it, beautiful, let me in. Let me make you feel good." I continue rubbing tight little circles on her bundle of nerves as I kiss down the front of her throat and in between her breasts. When the tip of my cock hits her barrier, I pause and look up at my queen. "This is it. There's no going back once I'm inside you."

"I want it. I want you. Make me yours, Razor."

I growl and drive forward, breaking through her innocence and sinking inside her snug pussy. She whimpers and I hold myself still, placing kisses up and down her neck, her jaw, her cheeks, and finally I take her lips in a long, languid kiss.

"Holy fuck," I grit out, burying my face into the crook of her shoulder. "So goddamn tight for me. Are you okay, Aurora?" I ask, lifting my head to look at her to make sure she's telling me the truth.

"So good. So full. I think I need... I think I'd like it if you moved."

I smirk at her adorable answer. "I think I'd like it if you told me what you want more often. I told you I'd give you anything."

"Right now I..."

"Yes, beautiful?" I ask, nipping her earlobe and sucking on that spot below her ear I know drives her crazy.

"Right now I want you to *fuck me*."

"Jesus," I mutter as more precum leaks out of my dick.

I pull all the way out and circle her entrance with the head of my cock. She whines and moves her hips, trying to get me where she wants me. Good. I need her to be certain she wants me, that she needs me as much as I need her.

I snap my hips and hit home in one long thrust. We both cry out at the sensations breaking over our bodies. I feel it, feel her blood pulsing in her veins, the air filling up her lungs, the muscles of her pussy sucking me in further than I thought I could go.

"You're so deep," Aurora whimpers, shifting her hips and spreading her legs wider for me, letting me fuck her just like she asked.

I grunt with each powerful thrust, grinding down then pulling almost all of the way out only to hammer into her again and again. I feel her cunt tightening around me as her cream coats my cock. She's fucking gushing for me, the wet, sloppy sounds filling the room along with the smell of our combined pleasure.

"Fucking hell, Aurora," I groan, angling my hips to find her g-spot. I know the instant I hit it. Her pussy clamps down on me as her breath hitches and her eyes squeeze shut. Aurora twists beneath me and cries out as her orgasm is ripped from her very core.

I slide my hands under her shoulders and pull her closer, shoving her down on my dick each time I hit home. I fuck her through her climax, pounding that sweet little pussy as she tenses and releases, shaking with pure bliss.

I give her a moment to rest, and then I roll on my back, taking her with me. Aurora places her hands on my chest to steady herself, her cunt still pulsing around my shaft.

"Ride my fucking cock, princess," I growl. I see a flash of insecurity cross her face, but I pull her down for a kiss so she doesn't spend another second doubting herself or her impact on me.

My hands slide up her thighs and grip her hips in a punishing hold. Together we find the right rhythm, creating a delicious ache with each roll of our hips. She feels incredible. Beneath me, on top of me, beside me, for the rest of our fucking lives.

"R-R-Razor..." she stutters out, her big tits swaying in front of my face as she rests her hands on either side of my head. I suck on her tits, lick her nipples, and scrape my teeth along her sensitive flesh.

I grab her ass, *hard*, and grind her pussy down on me while I fuck up into her, hitting her g-spot with every rough stroke. Aurora starts to tremble, her arms barely holding her up as we climb higher and higher.

"Come for me," I grit out, one hand still squeezing her ass while the other trails up her side and wraps firmly around her neck.

"Ohmygod," Aurora moans, her pussy pulsing as a flood of wetness pours over my cock, soaking the sheets beneath us.

I tighten my hold around her neck and dig my fingers into the flesh of her ass, forcing her to ride me hard. My spine tingles and my balls draw up tight, my dick swelling and throbbing inside of her warm, wet pussy.

"Come right now!" I roar as my thrusts grow erratic.

"I-I-I..."

I squeeze her throat and she fucking detonates, throwing her head back, screaming my name as tears pour down her flushed cheeks. My orgasm shoots through me, the sharp ecstasy stealing my breath as I empty myself inside her womb. It hurts so fucking good, feeling her walls choke my raw dick as rope after rope paints the inside of her pussy.

Aurora collapses, curling up on my chest and burying her face into the side of my neck. I wrap my arms around her, keeping her close as we stay connected like this, as close as two people can be.

"Are you okay?" I ask after a few hushed moments of catching our breath. Jesus, I lost my mind. "I said I'd be careful but I..."

"You said you'd take care of me," Aurora counters, tilting her head up so I can see her face. She has a cheeky little grin, which settles me down ever so much. I couldn't live with myself if I hurt her in any way. "After like a thousand orgasms, I'd say you lived up to your promise."

"Good," I tell her, kissing her forehead before getting her snuggled up against me once more.

Aurora kisses my neck while I rub her back, both of us soaking up whatever feeling this is between us. I know I've never felt it before, which only confirms my earlier suspicions; I'm head over fucking heels for this woman.

Eventually, we both start shivering from the sweat drying on our bodies. "Shower time?" I suggest.

"Together?!" comes her eager response. I groan and nuzzle into the side of her neck.

"As incredible as that sounds, I know I won't be able to keep my hands off you." I can tell she's about to say something to change my mind, but I keep pressing forward. "Your body needs to recover. Just a little bit." Aurora pouts, which is about the cutest and sexiest thing I've ever seen. "I promise, princess, we can fuck in every room, on every surface in this house." She nods, her eyes lighting up. Jesus, she's perfect. "But not right now. Rest. Heal. Relax." I kiss the tip of her nose, then crawl out of bed. "Do you want to go first?"

She shakes her head. "I don't think I can move yet." I smirk at her, and she returns it.

"I'll just hop in the shower then and you can go after. Or whenever. Make yourself at home, princess. That's where you are now."

Aurora nods, her eyes shining with warmth and love. I feel it, too. I just hope I'm able to prove it to her before this house of cards I've built comes crashing down.

Chapter 10

Aurora

I roll over in bed, stretching my deliciously sore muscles as I let out a contented sigh. I feel thoroughly used and completely satisfied. The water turns on for the shower, and I decide to get up and do some exploring while Razor is still in there.

I know I should be anxious about Viper and the Serpents, but right now, I can't keep the smile off my face. Razor makes me feel so safe and protected, I'm starting to believe him when he says he'll take care of me.

Still, my stomach twists when I think about Razor facing off with my brother's club. He said he's in the security business, but one man can only do so much when confronted with two dozen hardened criminals. What if I just brought the wrath of the Serpents to Razor's doorstep?

Razor will have a solution. I trusted him with my sketchy past and my pathetic present, maybe he'll be the one to give me a fulfilling future.

A chill sweeps over my naked body and I decide to throw on one of Razor's shirts while I continue my exploration. Opening the first drawer of his dresser, I find a pile of socks, none of them matching. I smile to myself, knowing this new piece of information about the man I'm already half in love with.

Moving on to the second dresser drawer, I open it, not believing my eyes. My smile drops right along with my stomach. The first shirt haphazardly strewn across the pile of other clothes in the drawer has a Rebel Hearts logo on it.

I reach out with a trembling hand, pausing when I'm a fraction of an inch away from the fabric as if it might burn me if I touch it. I have to know.

Grabbing the shirt, I hold it out in front of me, unable to breathe as I read *Rebel Hearts Motorcycle Club* scrawled beneath their logo. I'm frozen in place, my fingers growing numb from gripping the shirt so hard in my fists.

Maybe he got it at a second-hand store, I try justifying to myself.

Tossing the shirt on the bed behind me, I race to the closet and fling the double doors open. There, hanging right up front in all its glory, is a Rebel Hearts cut. There's no mistaking it and there's no way in hell he found this a thrift shop.

Oh god. Oh my god. *Oh my fucking god.*

I ran away from one club, right into the arms of another. More specifically, I fell into bed with a member "in security." I know what that means. Razor is the Enforcer. The one who roughs people up and intimidates their targets into getting information. The Enforcer for the Serpents is a brutal man with callouses and scars on his knuckles from the beatings he unleashes on his enemies.

Razor has never treated me like that, my heart tells me.

What do I even know about Razor, really? This is all a lie, my brain argues.

I slam my eyes shut and put my hands over my ears, feeling overstimulated and out of control. My mind races with possibilities and explanations that don't end with Razor lying to get me into bed.

He was there when I almost got hit by that car. He showed up right when I needed him last night, which means... he was already parked outside the compound. There's no other way he'd get to me so fast, let alone know where to find me.

"No," I whisper, tears clogging my throat and burning my eyes. But the truth is finally setting in.

I drop my hands from my face, my entire body shaking with rage and betrayal.

Razor has been stalking me, or at least stalking the club, and used my escape as an opportunity to exploit not only me but the club. That's the only thing that makes sense. He wanted to humiliate my brother by using me.

Do I really believe that? The man I've gotten to know isn't manipulative or violent. Then again, anyone can put on a show for a few days. He pretended to be nice to me, he even listened to me spill my heart out about everything that happened to me, and the whole time, he was probably dying with laughter inside.

What a fool I've been. A complete idiot. A naive woman desperately seeking belonging and human touch. I went and trusted the first man to show me an ounce of kindness, only to have it blow up in my face.

I listen for the sound of the shower, nodding to myself when I hear it still running. I grab my beer-soaked clothes from last night, which are dry by now, but still smelly and disgusting. Hesitating for a moment, I debate on whether to steal some of Razor's clothes but decide I don't want anything of his.

I cringe as I step into my shorts and pull on my shirt, my nose wrinkling against the assault of stale beer and cigarette smell. Even so, this is a better option than staying here. Gathering up the rest of my scant belongings, I make a run for the front door, leaping down the porch steps and letting my feet carry me anywhere but here.

After a few minutes of turning down one street corner and then another, I slow to a walking pace. I was starting to draw attention, which is the last thing I want.

Shit. Now what? The Rebel Hearts will be after me soon, as well as the Serpents. I mean, what the hell? How did my life come to this? I never should have left the compound. Viper was right, I can't survive without the club, whether I like it or not.

It's not quite noon yet, which means the majority of the members are still passed out or groggily waking up and stumbling back home. They might not have even noticed I was gone, or if they did, maybe they forgot in their drunken stupors.

Am I really going back?

What other choice do I have?

I fought so hard to be free...
And once I was, I ran right into another prison.

I take a deep breath and blow it out, accepting my fate. Better to go with the devil you know, right? At least, that's how the saying goes.

Taking a moment to get my bearings, I plot out the fastest route on foot to the Serpents' compound. Good thing Maplewood is a small town and Main Street is never more than a few blocks away. Once I get there, it'll be a straight shot to the compound.

I'm sweaty and exhausted by the time I get to the old farmhouse. Leaning against the outside wall next to the back door, I take a moment to calm down and paste on my usual smile. I just need to pretend that nothing happened. I didn't run away last night and give my virginity to a member of a rival club. That would be crazy. Reckless. Idiotic.

When I've waited as long as I dare without going unnoticed, I straighten my shoulders and hold my head high as I step into the kitchen of the clubhouse. Brandi is there, though instead of the strapless dress she was wearing the night before, she has a torn sweatshirt, undoubtedly from whichever member she slept with last night. For the first time in my life, I can relate to Brandi.

It's not a good feeling.

She turns, looking me up and down before frowning. "Rough night?" she asks, though I can tell she's already lost interest. Fine by me.

"Something like that," I reply with a smile. Brandi waves me off before grabbing a half-empty bottle of whiskey. She disappears into the shadows, crawling back into bed with a wake-up drink for her man, I guess.

I sneak out of the kitchen, peering into the catastrophic mess that was left in the bar area last night. Usually, I'd have most of it cleaned up by now.

"Where the fuck have you been?" Viper snarls from behind me as he grabs my upper arm. My brother yanks me backward and spins me around, making me stumble.

"I w-wasn't feeling w-well l-last night," I lie. I've never been great at hiding the truth, unlike all the men in my life, apparently. "I went to bed early," I say with more confidence this time. "It must have been a migraine or something. I just woke up and came here as soon as I realized how late I slept."

Viper stares at me, his usually dead eyes flickering with something dark. He's always had a temper, which the drugs made worse. But this look... It's obsessive and lustful, though not toward me. He's on a power trip, his focus solely on money, drugs, and controlling this town. This new partnership with the cartel has him hungry for more. For everything.

I'm worried he won't believe me, but after a moment, Viper nods his head. "Go clean yourself up," he grunts. "You look disgusting." My brother spits on me, his saliva landing on my shoulder.

"I will," I promise, taking a step to the side so I can go back to the storage shed I converted into a studio apartment across the gravel lot.

"I have a special project for you today. Need you to do a solid for the club."

I swallow thickly, a pit forming in my stomach. Still, I nod, agreeing to whatever he says just so I can get out of here.

"Come find me in my office," Viper instructs. His "office" is a room upstairs with a safe full of cash and a table with lines of cocaine ready to snort at any given moment.

Only when he stomps down the hall and heads upstairs do I let go of the breath I was holding. I don't have a good feeling about this. Maybe I should have tried my luck confronting Razor or run to the nearest railroad track and jumped on the first train moving slowly enough for me to catch.

None of that matters anymore. I'm locked in now.

Twenty minutes later, I emerge from my apartment with clean clothes and freshly washed hair. A wave of sadness breaks over my body at the thought of how I wanted to join Razor in the shower this morning. Another wave washes over me, this one bringing despair and betrayal with it. Finally, anger settles in.

Entering the clubhouse once more, I get a few glares from the club bunnies as I walk past the bar area. Viper must have told them to earn their keep by cleaning up once in a while. That's what he does on the very rare occasion I'm unable to do all of the chores and cleaning in one morning.

I have bigger things to worry about than the ire of Brandi, Danielle, and the other girls. For all I know, this *special project* could get me killed. At least I wouldn't have to deal with the bunny drama or the consequences of sleeping with the enemy.

Wow, that's a dark thought.

"There you are," Viper says, wiping his nose and sniffling a few times. There's still some white powder on the side of his left nostril, but I'm certainly not going to be the one to point that out to him.

I stand silently in the doorway, waiting for his next command.

"Don't look so stiff and awkward," my brother barks out, making me jump. "I need you to be cool and calm for this. It's no big deal, so there's no reason to be nervous."

Nodding, I keep my eyes focused on the floor. I don't want to look at Chad. At what he's become; a terrifying addict ruled by power and surrounded by drug paraphernalia, dirty money, and stolen goods.

"Rory," he says, his voice softer than I've heard in a long time.

I finally look up at him, watching as my brother stands from his seat and walks over to me. He hasn't called me Rory since we were kids. It was his nickname for me. No one else called me Rory. Only Chad.

"You trust me, right? I'm your big brother. I've protected you your entire life. I'd never put you in danger."

A thousand memories of my childhood flood my mind. Chad distracting me from our parents fighting, us playing in the park, him teaching me how to ride a bike, and then promptly teaching me how to bandage up a scraped knee.

But the man standing in front of me today isn't Chad. He's Viper. I've suffered his wrath physically and emotionally over the years. I've dealt with his mood swings, his erratic behavior, and his excessive drug use, all while keeping the clubhouse in order.

I know he's manipulating me, but I'm powerless to do anything about it.

"I know," I say, sounding more confident than I feel.

"Good," he replies with a smile. This isn't the pleasant, happy smile of Chad. It's the sly, wicked smirk of a man with evil intentions. "All you have to do is take this backpack to some friends of mine in Dallas."

I may be stupid when it comes to love and relationships if the last twenty-four hours have proven anything, but I'm not a total idiot. I know there are drugs in the backpack. Several kilos of cocaine, if I'm not mistaken.

"I... don't know if–"

Viper snaps, his hand flying through the air and hitting my cheek with enough force to make me dizzy. His fingers wrap around my neck and he pulls me forward before slamming me against the wall.

"You *will* do this for me," he snarls, his nostrils flaring as he shakes with anger. I can hardly breathe, but I try shaking my head no. Viper tightens his grip, making me lightheaded. "Or else I'll have to find out where you really went last night. I have a feeling you don't want that."

"I'll do it," I manage to choke out.

Viper drops his hand from my throat and I collapse onto the ground, my hands pressing against the sides of my neck as I cough and suck down air.

"Stop being so dramatic," he says, clearly annoyed with my need to breathe. "There's a burgundy sedan out front I rented under a fake name. Here are the keys." Viper tosses them in my direction, hitting me in the chest. "I'll send the location to your phone. Don't fuck this up, Aurora. I may be the Vice President, but I only have so much say around here. If the big guy doesn't want you around because you won't contribute..."

Viper shrugs and holds his hands out, palms up, letting me fill in the blanks. If I don't do this, my secret and shameful affair will be discovered and my brother will make sure I'm silenced. For good.

"Are you deaf?" he shouts, his mood swinging from annoyance to rage at the drop of a hat. "I told you to get your ass in that fucking car and deliver that backpack. Go!"

I scramble to my feet, grabbing the backpack and slinging one strap over my shoulder.

Shit, this thing is heavy. I don't even want to think about how much cocaine I'm currently carrying through the clubhouse and outside into the front parking lot. If I stop to think about any of this, I'm going to lose my mind and do something stupid like ditch the backpack, drive up north, and just keep going and going until I run out of money and gas. Then again, the last time I ran away, I was betrayed in the worst way possible.

I set the backpack in the front seat, then decide to place it in the back. After looking at it through the window for a moment, I change my mind and put it back in the front, on the floor this time. *Does it really matter where the backpack is? If I'm pulled over or jumped, they'll find it anyway.*

Opening the driver's side door, I climb inside, adjusting the seat so it's more comfortable. Not that I'll ever be comfortable doing this, but at least my back won't be bent at a weird angle.

I set my phone on the dashboard and open up the message from Viper with the location. After plugging the address into my phone, I start up the directions. With trembling fingers, I raise the key to the ignition and turn, starting up the average-looking, bland car. I'm sure that was a purposeful choice.

I've walked and driven through Maplewood a hundred thousand times in my life, but never like this. I'm hyper-aware of everything and everyone I see. *Are they looking at me? Do they know? Am I driving too fast? Or not fast enough?*

I make it through the main part of town and turn onto a gravel road that runs alongside the major highway. I figured the less-traveled roads would have fewer cops. Then again, maybe it's more suspicious if I'm driving alone on a road that usually has no traffic. I don't fucking know, but the decision has been made.

I'm about to make a left turn out of town and follow this old country highway as far as I can before merging onto I-35, but the familiar rumble of motorcycle engines in the distance catches my attention. Are the Serpents following me to make sure I deliver the package? That doesn't make sense though.

Looking into my rearview mirror, my eyes widen in panic while my heart thuds painfully against my ribcage. It's not the Serpents. It's the Rebel Hearts.

I make the left turn, pressing the gas pedal down as far as it will go. Instead of zooming off like I thought I would, the tires spin in place, shooting loose gravel everywhere. The car fishtails across the intersection, the right back tire getting wedged and stuck in the mud on the side of the road.

The car comes to an abrupt halt, throwing my considerable weight against the seatbelt strapped across my chest. I'm sweating, shaking, and barely able to breathe with the fear and adrenaline pumping through my veins.

I'm stuck. Trapped. Even if I ran, they'd catch me. Do they want the drugs for themselves? What would Viper do if I came back empty-handed and told him his supply was stolen?

A loud tap against my window makes me shriek and spin around in my seat. I look up, up, up, seeing a tall man with blue eyes and dark brown hair. He has a Rebel Hearts cut on as well as a Rebel Hearts bandana. The patch on his cut lets me know he's the president.

I roll down my window before he shoots it out. I know how this works. I'm outnumbered, outgunned, and overpowered in every way. The man bends down and gets a good look at me, his eyes widening in surprise. He looks over his shoulder at the men surrounding him, giving them a questioning look.

"You sure this is the right car? I think we got some bad intel," the man says.

"My intel is spot on," another man says. "I don't give out bad information."

"What about the backpack?" someone else asks. I didn't realize they were surrounding my car. Two people are staring at the bag through the passenger side window. I shake my head no, which apparently was the wrong move.

"I knew it," the biker who gave the intel says, a hint of self-satisfaction in his voice.

I hit the lock button on the doors, but I'm too late. One of the men rips the car door open and grabs the backpack. I shut my eyes and wrap my arms around my stomach, hoping to keep myself from throwing up all over the inside of the car. Then again, maybe that would be just the distraction I need to get away.

"There's got to be at least ten kilos in here just judging from the weight," someone says.

More men talk and argue, but their voices are fading into the background as I fold in on myself. My heart is racing right along with my thoughts and I find it difficult to get a full breath while there's a vice crushing my lungs.

"Miss?" a voice says. I must have heard them wrong. "Uh, ma'am?" the voice says again. "Don't want you passing out on us. Can you take a few breaths?"

I don't understand what's happening.

"Seems like you found yourself in a bad situation," the first man, the president of the Rebel Hearts says. I nod, managing to look up at him through my window. He doesn't look like he's going to hit me or put a bullet in my head, so that's good. "Look, I can't just let you go. You're involved and we need to know how much."

I nod again, apparently unable to do anything else at the moment.

"Why don't you scoot over to the other seat and Tank here, our VP, will drive you over to our clubhouse."

It's not like I have a choice. I do as he asks, getting settled in the passenger seat while another large and intimidating man sits in the driver's seat. We're silent for the entire ride, which is good. I don't know what to say, what to tell, what to lie about. Where do my loyalties lie? Viper? The Serpents, who have always treated me like less than a human? Are the Rebel Hearts really as bad as my brother made them out to be? So far, they're treating me with more respect than anyone in the Serpents. Razor was never cruel to me, he was only ever understanding and calming.

My world has changed so much in the last day. I don't know where to go from here or where I'll be this time tomorrow. Thoughts, doubts, and fears swirl around in my brain, making me dizzy. I rest my head against the cool glass of the window, trying to decide if I even want to survive this.

Honestly? I don't know anything anymore.

Chapter 11

Razor

I burst into the Rebel Hearts clubhouse, which is an old converted warehouse at the end of a long driveway. My lungs are burning and my heart is racing right along with my mind.

I don't know exactly what made Aurora run but I have a pretty good idea. When I stepped out of the shower and walked the short distance to the bedroom, I was expecting to see my princess still sprawled out on the bed, possibly sleeping.

Instead, the room was empty. A Rebel Hearts shirt was spread out on the bed and my closet doors were open. I winced when I saw the first article of clothing was my cut. I usually wear it all the time, but I've had to be stealthier with all the stakeouts. And yes, I wanted to avoid the conversation with Aurora. I guess the secret is out now. I just have to find my woman and beg for her forgiveness before it's too late.

The place is surprisingly empty for this time of day. Usually, club members are mulling about, or at the very least, I can always find Aldis or Tank.

Did they call church? I would have gotten a call...

Pulling out my phone, I curse under my breath when I see it's dead. I should have thrown it on the charger earlier but I was a bit distracted. Shit.

I grunt in frustration as I stomp through the otherwise silent space. I checked it when I discovered Aurora was missing, but then realized I never even got her fuckin' phone number. How much of a jackass am I? Lying to Aurora, taking advantage of her vulnerability, and then not even having the decency to get her number? I have a lot to apologize for.

The backdoor of the clubhouse swings open, revealing several of my MC brothers. Tritan, Drak, and Aldis walk in, followed by Tank and...

Aurora? What the actual fuck?

I'm frozen in place as I watch my brothers march Aurora to the back. She looks absolutely petrified, shaking from head to toe and trying so damn hard not to cry. Everything in me shatters, knowing I caused this. I should have been honest from the beginning and had Aurora helping us all along. It seemed impossible at the time, but anything would've been better than this.

"Aurora!" I shout across the clubhouse. All four men and Aurora turn their heads, five sets of eyes staring at me, each with different looks on their faces. Aldis looks more confused than anything, while Drak looks pissed off.

Aurora... My princess looks absolutely stricken by betrayal. The tears she was holding back come rushing to the surface and she lets out a quiet sob that nearly has me collapsing on the floor with the weight of guilt and shame.

"You two know each other?" Aldis asks, his tone even. There's a reason he's our president. Aldis is naturally laid back, but he can be firm and commanding when he needs to be. Right now, he understands this is a delicate situation.

Aurora doesn't say anything but I nod.

"What the hell? How–"

"Let's take this somewhere more private," Aldis says, cutting off whatever Tank was going to say. I nod and follow everyone into the back room, where we usually hold church.

Tank has had his hand around Aurora's bicep this whole time, directing her where to go. I know Tank has a woman of his own that he's crazy about, but tell that to the jealousy rippling through my muscles.

Once we're all seated, Aldis starts the conversation with one word. "Explain."

"I was on a stakeout checking up on the cartel lead we got from that prospect," I say.

Aldis hums in acknowledgment while Aurora's eyes widen. She doesn't say anything but she must be so hurt right now. We met because I was, and am, trying to take her brother's club down. We met because I became obsessed and couldn't let her go. Now look where we are.

"Aurora was there that first night," I continue. "She was with the club, but not part of the club. I didn't know she was the VP's sister."

"You're Viper's sister?" Tank asks in surprise. "And he sent you on a drug run?"

Aurora hangs her head and sniffles, finally whispering, "Yes."

My woman feels ashamed of her actions, but I know what Tank was really trying to say. He's shocked and disgusted that Viper used his sister, his own flesh and blood, as bait. He either knew we'd intercept or he didn't care. Maybe he didn't even think about us at all, and really sent his little sister straight into the drug den of the cartel.

"Piece of shit," Tank grunts. Aurora jumps and I'm out of my chair in a second, wanting, no, needing to comfort her.

She shrinks away from me, which feels like being slammed in the chest by a wrecking ball. "You're not in trouble," I tell her. I want to scoop her up and carry her away from here so we can talk in private, but we're not done here yet.

I take my seat once more and tell my MC brothers as well as Aurora how my infatuation started. My words are clunky and awkward as I try to describe how I was compelled to follow her. At first, it was for the club, but then it was just for me.

"I should have told you sooner," I say to Aurora, who never took her eyes off me the entire time. "And I should have clued you guys in," I confess, looking from Aldis to Tank. "I didn't know how to... I didn't even know if there would be anything to tell. It all happened so fast and–"

Aldis holds his hand up, effectively silencing me without a word.

"Your turn, Aurora. Tell me how you ended up in a car with ten kilos of coke headed toward Dallas."

Aurora swallows thickly and clears her throat. I lean forward in my seat, hanging on her every word.

"When I got back to the Serpents' clubhouse after..." she trails off, her eyes cutting to me and then back to Aldis. "Anyway, when I got back, Viper said he had a special project for me. He didn't take it well when I tried to tell him no."

Aurora rubs her cheek which I notice for the first time is red and swollen. Continuing my search, I notice angry red fingerprints on the side of her neck.

"He hit you?" I growl, unable to contain my rage.

Aurora shrugs. "I should have seen it coming," she responds matter-of-factly. I don't like that answer or what it implies. "It wasn't the violence that made me cave," she goes on. "I don't... I don't have anything outside of the Serpents. As much as I loathe cleaning up after their parties and taking whatever verbal or physical assaults they throw my way, what other choice do I have? They'd never let me leave. Not alive, at least. Viper made that crystal clear. Do the drop-off or..."

She lets the thought hang in the air while adrenaline mixes with rage and sorrow in the pit of my stomach. How fucking dare he treat Aurora this way? The abuse, the threats, the danger he put her in.

"I'm so sorry," I say, not caring that my brothers are here. I stand from my seat and kneel in front of Aurora, holding out my hands for her to take. She hesitates, her hazel eyes glistening with tears. "If I could go back and tell you the truth so you never would have run away, I would. I didn't know if you'd leave me after finding out my affiliation with the Rebel Hearts. I was selfish and wanted to keep you all to myself in our little fantasy world. But I don't just want the fantasy, Aurora."

My girl finally rests her hands in mine, letting me hold them while I continue. I'm on a roll now and I need to push through otherwise the words and courage might leave me altogether.

"I want the reality. I want you here with me, by my side. I want to show you off to my friends, my brothers and let them know you've been claimed. I want you as mine, Aurora."

"Yours?" she asks tentatively.

I nod. "We're partners. I don't own you like I imagine the men of the Serpents treat their women. But you're mine to protect. Mine to cherish. Mine to love."

Aurora's eyes flash with surprise, followed by tears. Fuck. I fucked it all up. I lost her. I–

"You love me?"

"Yes," I answer automatically. "With all of me. I know we have more to discuss and I have more apologizing to do, but you need to know I'm all in. You were never a pawn to me, princess. You're my whole world. Will you forgive me for keeping this secret from you? For putting you through all of this?"

I wait with bated breath, putting my own rebellious heart on the line for her to either throw away or treasure forever.

"If you don't forgive him, I will," Triton says, breaking the tension.

Aurora smiles for the first time in so damn long. It's small and a bit shaky, but it's there all the same.

"I love you, too," she whispers.

"Say it again," I demand, needing to hear those words a hundred more times. A thousand. It'll never be enough.

"I love you, Razor. I understand why you didn't tell me. It hurt like hell to find out the way I did, but I don't blame you for what my brother made me do. His actions are his own, just like mine are. And right now, I just want to go home. With you."

I nod and pull her up from her seat, wrapping my arms around her while she buries her face into my shoulder.

"As touching as this is, we still have a few details to work out," Tank says, keeping us on track.

I sigh in annoyance, making Aurora giggle softly. The sound travels all the way down inside my soul, settling there and warming me from the inside out.

We sit and discuss the next steps. The Serpents won't be expecting Aurora back for another couple of hours, which leaves a window of opportunity where they will be vulnerable. Taking down the Serpents, burning their clubhouse, and confiscating their weapons, money, and drugs won't eliminate the threat of the cartel for good, but it will destroy the foothold they have and the tentative partnership with the Serpents. We get to live to fight another day and eradicate drugs from Maplewood. That's about as happy of an ending as these things have.

Aldis comes up with a plan of attack and starts calling the appropriate members to make it happen. I'm torn between riding with them to exact my revenge on the fucking scumbag that is Viper and staying with my girl to make sure she's okay.

The president senses the battle I'm having and makes the decision for me. "Thank you both for telling the truth. Eventually," he says, giving me a look. We'll be talking later, of that I'm sure. For now, I have my girl and my club. That's all a man like me can hope for. "The guys and I will handle it from here. You two head on home and recover. I'll update you when it's done."

I nod and gather up Aurora in my arms, carrying her, bridal-style, through the clubhouse and out to my bike. I help her on, instructing her to hold on tight as I start up the engine. My bike roars to life and Aurora clings to me, resting her cheek on my back. Each passing moment with my girl on the back of my bike heals my raw, bruised heart.

We pull into my driveway and I help Aurora off the bike, wrapping an arm around her when her knees wobble.

"I've actually never ridden on a motorcycle before," she admits, her voice a little shaky. "Crazy, huh?"

My girl peers up at me, her hazel eyes an intoxicating mix of green and blue at the moment. "I'm glad I could be your first," I tell her. She gives me the sweetest smile, no doubt remembering all the other firsts she's experienced with me. "Now let's get inside, love. We'll finally take that shower together, yeah?"

Aurora nods and leans into me while we walk inside and head toward the bathroom. We take our time undressing and heating up the shower, and then I lead her inside. Gently, so damn gently, I begin cleaning my sweet princess with a washcloth and soap.

When we're done, I dry her off and wrap her in a fluffy towel before grabbing a towel for myself. I guide Aurora to the bedroom, sensing how exhausted she is. She sits on the bed while I turn around and dig through my drawers for a shirt she can wear. By the time I turn around, she's already curled up on her side with her eyes closed. Her towel fell off, leaving her exposed to my hungry eyes.

Not right now, I tell myself. She's been through so much the last twenty-four hours and she needs her rest.

Chuckling to myself at how adorable she is, I decide to forego clothing as well, opting instead to crawl into bed next to her. I carefully remove the towel from where she was lying on it and use it to pat her hair dry. I don't want her getting cold or having tangles in her hair when she wakes up.

When I'm satisfied that she's all taken care of, I pull the covers up over us and curl my naked body around hers. Aurora sighs contentedly in her sleep, mending my heart even further. She trusts me, even after everything I did.

The last thought I have before drifting to sleep is that I'm never letting Aurora go.

I'm not sure how much time has passed, but it's dark when I open my eyes. I must have dozed off right along with my sweet girl. What woke me up?

Aurora moans softly in her sleep, wiggling her hips to get closer to me. Fuck me, my princess is having a filthy dream. I can't stop the deep, hungry growl rising up from my chest when she adjusts her leg and grazes my hard as fuck dick. She's still asleep, but her leg hooks around mine, her knee rubbing up against my nearly painful erection.

I reach down and wrap my hand around the back of her knee. I meant to push her leg away so I don't come all over myself like a teenager, but instead, I find myself grinding against her. I sink my teeth into my bottom lip as unbelievable pleasure rolls through me. How can I be so close to the edge from just this simple touch?

But I already know the answer. It's her. Everything about her. I'll never get enough. I know I need to stop, but god, she feels so damn good. Precum leaks out of me, my raging hard-on needing some kind of relief. When Aurora rubs her pussy up against my thigh, I groan loudly, unable to contain the sound.

Aurora returns my groan with one of her own, awareness slowly creeping into her movements as she wakes up. Her nails bite into my bare chest, snapping the last thread of my control. Wrapping her long hair around my fist, I tilt her head back, growling when I see her hazel eyes ablaze. My lips are on hers in the next second.

I swallow down her cries of pleasure as I devour her. Her hot, curvy little body writhes against mine, creating delicious, torturous friction. I need more. Need to feel her from the inside out. Need to consume her, taste her sweat, bite her soft skin, and drink down everything she's offering. After almost losing her earlier today, I need to know she's still here. Still mine.

"Razor," she whimpers into my mouth before capturing my lips once more. I pull her on top of me so she's straddling my lap. Aurora breaks our kiss, gasping for air. "Razor," she says again as she rolls her hips.

Jesus, her pussy lips wrap around my cock, the wet heat driving me insane. I've never had this overwhelmingly primal need to fuck, to claim, to possess someone completely. Aurora rests her forehead on mine as a shudder ripples through her curves. I know she's as desperate as I am when a pained whimper escapes her mouth.

She sits up, steadying herself with both hands on my chest. I grip her hips and lift her up, positioning her dripping wet hole over the head of my cock. I hiss out a breath and squeeze my eyes shut, trying with everything in me not to come like this. Her cunt pulses, massaging my sensitive dick and making me buck my hips involuntarily and slide a few inches inside of her.

"Are you sure, baby?" I grit out, though I pray to god she doesn't stop. I'd never take what she doesn't offer, but goddamn, I'm in physical pain every single second I'm not inside of her.

Instead of answering, Aurora bites her bottom lip and nods, her big, brilliant eyes telling me everything I need to know. Slowly, so slowly, Aurora sinks down on my length, her pussy stretching obscenely wide around my cock.

I drag my eyes up her body, taking in her pale skin and silky blonde hair. She's practically glowing in the moonlight streaming through the window. I watch in awe as the silver light kisses the side of her face, her breasts, and her thighs. My fingers skim over everywhere the light touches, needing to feel this goddess as she brings me unimaginable pleasure.

Aurora tilts her head back and claws down my chest, gasping for air once she's fully seated. I grip her hips, anchoring her to me, keeping her right here. Her pussy flutters around my cock, making the fucker jerk and leak more precum inside of her.

"You feel so good," I whisper, unable to find my voice as I get lost in the way our bodies are connected on every level.

I help her find her rhythm, rolling her hips and grinding her down on my swollen dick. Each movement sends sharp pangs of ecstasy shooting through my veins. I know she feels it, too, with each breathy whimper that falls from her lips.

Aurora's eyes snap open, locking on mine. I see the moment she recognizes her power. Her strength. Those hazel-green eyes shift to a fierce blue, making my normally sweet girl almost feral as she lifts up on her knees and drops down on me, her cunt swallowing my dick completely.

An animalistic growl rumbles through her, wracking her body as she fucks me furiously. Christ, it's all I can do to hold on. I want this for her, need this, need her to take control and understand that I'm hers. She owns me, body and soul.

I cup the back of her neck and pull her down for a kiss, tasting her sweetness as she brings both of us closer, closer, closer...

"Razor," she whispers. "Razor... Razor... fuck..." Her whimpers turn into moans, louder, louder until she's crying out my name, her voice broken as she comes all around my cock. Goddamn, she comes with her whole body, every muscle tensing and releasing as her orgasm works its way through her.

I keep her right here with me, her forehead resting on mine as she shakes and releases more of her juices. Her hot, sticky cum drips down my dick and coats my balls... and holy hell, is she coming again? Aurora buries her face into the side of my neck, muffling her scream as an intense orgasm rips through her body.

Something breaks loose inside me, leaving me unhinged and wild with need. I flip Aurora onto her back and rut into her still-spasming pussy, grunting with each thrust. She bows her back and wraps her legs around my hips, digging her heels into my ass.

I lean down and suck on her breast, teasing one nipple and then the other, back and forth until I feel her fingernails bite into the back of my head. She pulls my hair and tilts my head up before slamming her mouth down on mine.

My greedy girl rocks into me, meeting me frantic thrust for frantic thrust. I break our kiss and inhale sharply, feeling my orgasm barrel through me. With a roar, I let go of every fucking thing and come so damn hard I feel my bones rattle.

Aurora's cries carve through the night air as her pussy snaps around me, milking me and prolonging our pleasure. We're both shaking and panting as we cling to each other, riding out the last of our orgasms.

I collapse on top of her, gathering her limp body up in my arms. I try rolling to the side to keep from crushing her, but Aurora urges me to stay right where I am. I'll be her safety blanket whenever she needs it. We stay wrapped up like that for long moments, Aurora taking deep breaths while I whisper how much she means to me and that she's safe right here in my arms.

Eventually, her grip on me loosens, allowing me to roll onto my back and drape her over my chest. We fall back into blissful sleep after connecting on the deepest level humanly possible.

Chapter 12

Aurora

"If I divide the fraction by three and find the common denominator..."

I type my answer into the practice test I've been working on all morning, giving myself a pat on the back when the answer pops up as correct. I started online classes last month, though I'm not sure what degree I want. I'm just getting back to the basics right now, including math. It's not my best subject, but I'm pushing through. I know I just need the credit so I can move on to other classes.

Razor steps into the living room, breaking my concentration without even saying a word. I'm always distracted when he's around. Even after being together for two months, I still get butterflies when those dark eyes lock onto mine.

"There you are, princess," he says in his deep, raspy voice. I smile at him and put my notebook and study material aside, patting the seat next to me on the couch.

He sits next to me, throwing his arm over the back of the couch so I can scoot closer. Razor has been working on a new addition to the house for more room. He didn't have to say it explicitly, but I know what that means. He's planning on starting a family with me, and I for one, can't wait to tell him our first child is already on the way. I took the test this morning and have been waiting for the right moment to surprise him.

"How's math going? I know it's not your favorite thing to work on."

"Actually, this is perfect timing..." I purr, clearing off the couch and then slowly climbing into Razor's lap, straddling him. "I was thinking I could use a study break," I whisper while grinding my already soaking pussy down on his growing erection. I can't help it. I already want him all the time, but these pregnancy hormones are no joke. My want has turned into a need.

"Oh fuck, baby," he groans, leaning in for a kiss. I pull back at the last moment and watch Razor pout. It's ridiculously cute.

I slip down Razor's lap and sink to my knees in front of him, grabbing at his belt before he can convince me otherwise. He always insists on making me cum first, and don't get me wrong, it's generous and incredible and amazing. But sometimes a girl just wants to pleasure her man.

Razor tangles his fingers in my hair and bends forward to try and kiss me again. I allow him one small peck, but then I place my hand on his chest and make him look me in the eye. "You've already given me so much, now let me."

He grins and then groans as I palm his cock over his jeans. I work his belt and zipper in no time and then pull out his glorious dick. It still shocks me every time I see it. He's *so* big, I'm amazed every single time that he even fits inside of me.

"Princess, if you keep looking at my dick like that, I'm gonna come in your hands," he grits out.

I smirk at him, biting my lip as I slowly stroke him with both hands.

"Jesus," he grunts.

Bending down, I lick the tip of his cock and dip my tongue inside the little slit on top. Razor hisses out a breath and throws his head back. I kiss the head of his shaft and then lick up and down his length, paying careful attention to the thick, throbbing vein on the underside of his dick.

His fingers tangle in my hair and he fists my strands while guiding me back to the tip of his cock, letting me know what he needs. My mouth opens automatically and I swallow him down, moaning as I suck him deep into my mouth.

"Aurora, god, baby. You're incredible."

I respond by opening up even more for him, taking him into my throat, and gagging on his huge dick. Razor grunts and snaps his hips, fucking my mouth while he holds me still. I love it. Love when he uses me for his pleasure. I know he's going to give it all back to me when we're done, but I'm not even focused on that right now. All I can concentrate on is the way my lips stretch around his girth.

"Shit, I'm not gonna last, love," he warns.

I moan around him and feel him twitch, precum dripping into my mouth as I suck him down. I reach out and massage his balls, giggling when he tenses up and swears loudly. I suck him faster, harder, rougher, slobbering all over his cock and squeezing his balls.

He grunts like an animal and then roars as he empties jet after jet of cum down my throat. I continue massaging him with my tongue until he pulls me off of him and slams his mouth down on mine.

I have to break the kiss to pull air into my oxygen-deprived lungs. Razor continues kissing up and down my neck, only breaking away from me so he can pull down my yoga pants.

"No panties?" he growls.

I shake my head no and smile seductively at him. In one swift move, Razor has me over his shoulder, my bare ass up in the air as he shuffles with his pants still on and his dick swinging between his legs. I laugh at his eagerness to get to the bedroom.

"I need to be inside that sweet pussy of yours," he growls as he tosses me down on the bed. My breasts jiggle as I hit the mattress and Razor's eyes lock on them, his pupils blown wide with lust. "Damn, beautiful. You're a fucking goddess. I can't believe you're mine."

I smile up at him, watching as he strokes himself. I grab my tits and twist my nipples, my legs spreading wide open in invitation. Razor kneels down beside the bed and grabs my ankles, pulling me toward him until my ass is on the edge of the bed.

"Fuck, look how wet you are for me, baby. Does giving your man pleasure turn you on?"

"God yes, Razor. So much."

He grunts and then dives into my pussy, making me moan as he laps up my juices. There's nothing sweet or tender about the way he's devouring me. Razor nips at my clit, making me jump and tense. His tongue and teeth work me over, driving me higher, higher, higher, close, so close, one more lick...

I shake with the need for release, my entire body strung tight as my back arches trying to get him right where I need him. Razor plunges two fingers into my dripping cunt and bites down on my clit.

I snap, screaming his name and gushing all over him. He licks me, sucks me, feasts on me even as wave after wave of ecstasy pulses through my body, taking me under, washing me away until I'm floating, falling, finished.

Not giving me much time to enjoy my blissful, post-orgasm bliss, Razor flips me on my stomach and pulls my hips up so I'm on all fours. He smacks my ass and massages away the sting. With a grunt, he enters me in one stroke, thrusting his dick deep inside of me.

He growls and pulls out, making me whimper.

"You need this cock? Need me to fuck you nice and hard?"

"Yes! Please, god, please fuck me."

"Love when you beg for it, beautiful. Sexiest goddamn thing in the world."

With that, he grabs my ass cheeks and spreads me wide open, slamming his fat cock in and out of me again and again. I can't catch my breath, he's pounding me so hard. He's merciless in the way he stretches me, breaks me, destroys me. I fist the sheets and scream as my orgasm rips through me.

"That's it, milk my fucking cock, dirty girl," He grits out, fucking me right through my orgasm, never letting up.

I'm raw, throbbing, and so, so sensitive, but I need more. Each stroke gives me a sharp pleasure bordering on pain, but I need it. I push back into him and swivel my hips. We both cry out as he wedges his dick deeper inside of me and grinds down, hitting my special spot with the head of his cock.

I'm right there, so close I can taste it, so close my pussy starts pulsing, so close I hold my breath and wait for the burst of bliss to rock through me.

But then Razor pulls out.

"Nooo!" I cry out. It's almost painful to not have him in me, to not have him give me my release.

Razor chuckles, though there's no humor in his voice. No, this is my wicked, filthy Razor who can't get enough of me. I love it.

He flips me over again so I'm on my back. Razor grabs my thighs and spreads me wide open, dragging his cock up and down my soaking wet slit, but never entering me. I whimper and beg and writhe beneath him.

Razor bends down and licks the sweat from between my breasts, trailing his tongue up to the hollow of my neck before biting me there softly.

"Tell me what you want, Aurora. Tell me how I can worship your gorgeous fucking body," Razor whispers in my ear as he continues to tease me.

I draw a shaky breath and turn my head to kiss him. Razor quickly takes over, breathing me in, tasting me, consuming me. His kiss is everything, all of his love, his commitment, his urgent need. It's somehow both sweet and savage. It's perfect.

When we finally break apart, I dig my nails into his back, making him growl.

"Fuck me, Razor. I need to come," I moan.

"Anything for you."

With that, he thrusts into me, making obscene noises as he fucks his huge cock in and out of my dripping cunt. Razor snaps his hips and tears me apart from the inside out. He grunts each time he hits home.

I feel that coil winding up deep inside, each stroke making it tighter, tighter, tighter...

Razor reaches a hand in between us and rubs furious circles over my clit until I snap, moaning his name, coming again and again around his thick dick. He pinches my clit while I'm at the peak of my climax and a sudden intense pressure releases deep inside of me, pain and pleasure pierce me through and through.

"Jesus, fuck, love, you just... Fuck, you squirted all over me."

I don't know what that means, but Razor seems to love it.

I bury my face in Razor's neck and bite him there, claiming him as mine. Clinging to his tense frame, I dig my nails into his back and hang on as my body is wrung dry. Razor roars his release, pumping in and out of me until my pussy is overflowing with his cum. I feel it trickle down my slit, the sensation overwhelming me and making me contract around him again.

Razor collapses on top of me, a sweaty, sated mess. He rolls us over and drapes me across his chest. We don't say anything just yet, both of us soaking in the silence, the calm, the beauty of the afterglow.

"That was amazing, baby. So good," he says, breaking the silence with a kiss to my temple.

"Mmhmm," I say, still trying to find my voice. This feels like the right moment to tell him my big news, so I shore up the courage and lean up on his chest so we're face to face.

Razor smiles at me so tenderly and tucks my hair behind my ear. God, this man. He can be so ferocious while we fuck, but so tender afterward. He's perfect and he's all mine.

"Something on your mind, beautiful?"

I nod and bite my lip, savoring this moment before I tell him my secret.

"I'm pregnant," I whisper.

Razor's eyes go wide with surprise, and then they fill with tears. A huge smile breaks out on his handsome face before he kisses away the tears that started to fall down my cheeks. He gently rolls us over so I'm on my back while he holds himself above me.

He dips his head down and kisses me so sweetly, then rests his forehead on mine. "We're having a baby," he whispers, kissing my jaw, my neck, my collarbone.

"Yeah," I whisper, shuddering as Razor continues to place feather-light kisses down my chest until he gets to my breasts.

He nuzzles his head there and breathes in deep. Razor looks up at me in awe from between my breasts. "These are gonna fill up with milk," he rasps, sucking on one nipple and then the other.

"Oh," I moan softly. It feels so, *so* good.

"Are they sensitive already?"

I nod and tangle my fingers in his hair, holding him in place. Razor licks, kisses, teases my nipples and my breasts until I'm shaking with need.

Taking his time, Razor continues trailing kisses down my ribcage until he gets to my belly. He rests his forehead there, rolling it back and forth and breathing me in.

"I love you. I love you both with everything I am," he whispers, kissing all over my belly.

"We love you too," I tell him.

Razor leans up and braces himself on his forearms, one on either side of my head. I feel his cock nudging my entrance, and I spread myself wide open for him.

"You're already...?"

"Hard? Yeah, princess. I'm always ready to slide inside of your beautiful, perfect body."

He enters me gently this time, rocking in and out of me and staring into my eyes. We're both crying, tears of happiness and love as Razor continues to fill me and build us both up. He kisses me softly, slowly, one drugging kiss leading to another and another.

I gasp as I come around him, my orgasm rippling through my body, lingering on my nerves, and then spiking again when I feel his warm release fill me up.

Razor turns us so we're lying on our sides, facing each other, his forehead resting on mine as he runs his fingers up and down my curves.

"I never thought I'd have this," he admits softly.

"Me either," I reply. "But I'm so happy we found each other. Well, technically, you found me."

Razor grins and presses a kiss on one cheek and then the other before settling back down again. I curl up against his chest, humming with contentment. My big, burly, secretly sweet, and funny man strokes his fingers down my back in a soothing gesture.

"We're having a baby," Razor whispers in awe.

"We sure are," I confirm.

"Let's talk names," Razor says, surprising me. "I've always thought Silas was a cool boy's name. And Gretta for a girl."

I smile at his eagerness. "Silas can be a contender but I'm not so sure about Gretta."

Razor and I talk about baby names and nursery decor until both of us yawn. I snuggle back down into my man's arms, feeling safe, loved, and excited about my future for the first time in my life.

Epilogue

Razor

"Silas! Don't go too far!" I shout as my eldest son takes off on his bicycle. I watch our ten-year-old speed up the block and take a right turn. No more than two minutes later, Silas has made it around the block and comes to a stop in front of me.

"Can I go again, Dad?" he asks, his brown eyes matching mine.

I remember having a lot of energy at his age, too. I was always amped up to do something but was yelled at to calm down and shut up by parents still coming down from a bad trip. My son will never know what that feels like as long as I'm around.

"Sure, buddy. Stick to our block, okay? Make sure to check in with either your mother or me at least every fifth time you go around," I say with a wink.

Silas tears off once more, lifting off the seat so he can stand and pump the pedals harder and go as fast as possible. God help us when he gets his first motorcycle. It's inevitable. The kid loves going on rides with me. He even rode with me in our bi-annual Poker Run Charity last year.

"I assume our son is as wound up as ever?" my wife asks from the front porch.

I look at her over my shoulder and then turn to face her fully. She's more beautiful now than when I met her, which is saying something. Her long golden hair flows behind her while those hazel eyes shine with love and playfulness.

My gaze wanders down her luscious curves, pausing to appreciate her full, round breasts and slightly rounded belly. Aurora just found out last month that we're expecting again - our fourth child. I'm still gunning for Gretta as a name, but mostly just to get a rise out of my gorgeous wife.

"Always," I finally answer as I make my way up to the porch.

I press a kiss to Aurora's forehead, then stand behind her and wrap my arms around my precious woman. She leans back against my shoulder, her lips tickling my neck. We stay like that for a few moments, laughing quietly when Silas zooms past us on his bike.

"I love you," she whispers. "I love our lives. Our kids. Our home. I never thought I'd have this."

I remember when I told Aurora the same thing right after she said she was pregnant. I didn't think life could get any better, but here I am, father of four, husband to the most incredible woman ever, and still going strong with the Rebel Hearts.

"We built this together," I murmur. "We took all the ugly, difficult, painful things in our past and turned them into a beautiful life."

Aurora nods and I turn my head, rubbing my nose against hers in the way I know she loves. "I can't wait to see what's next," she says softly.

"Me either," I confirm, my hand sliding down to her belly where our baby is growing. "Whatever the future holds, I'm just happy to have you by my side," I tell her. We sway back and forth, taking in the cool spring evening breeze and watching the sun slowly sink into the sky. I don't know what I did to deserve this, but I sure as hell won't give it up for anything.

Connect with me!

Check out my website, cameronhart.net[1], for sneak previews on my latest projects.

Follow me on social media:

Facebook Page - facebook.com/cameronhartauthor
    Instagram - instagram.com/cameron.hart.author
    TikTok - tiktok.com/@author.cameron.hart
    Goodreads - goodreads.com/16081533.Cameron_Hart
    Bookbub - bookbub.com/authors/cameron-hart

---

1. https://cameronhart.net/

9 798227 335135